"You *must* marry me."

Charles spoke more gently and reached for Elizabeth's hand. She jerked it away.

"No! I am persuaded that it is not necessary," she cried.

Charles had remained fairly calm up to this point, but he now became impatient. "You might at least consider *my* feelings in the matter. For I'll tell you, my girl, that I don't intend to have it said of me that I compromised you and did not marry you!"

Her chin lifted stubbornly. "I suppose I should feel honoured that you are willing to make such a sacrifice on my behalf, but I cannot allow it. At any rate, I should think that your reputation as a rake could only be enhanced."

"Don't be idiotic!" was his terse rejoinder. "And if your chin gets any higher, you are going to have a permanent crick in your neck!"

They sat there exchanging glares, until, unexpectedly, Charles began to laugh. It was not long before Elizabeth joined him and they both collapsed in helpless mirth.

If only we could stay this way, thought Elizabeth. But she knew that was like wishing after stars.

THE THOROUGHLY COMPROMISED BRIDE

CATHERINE REYNOLDS

Harlequin Books

TORONTO • NEW YORK • LONDON
AMSTERDAM • PARIS • SYDNEY • HAMBURG
STOCKHOLM • ATHENS • TOKYO • MILAN

With loving thanks to my four children,
Linda, Carl, Karen and Eric,
for all their enthusiasm and encouragement,
especially Linda and Eric,
who put up with me while I created
And a special thanks to Joan Hayter,
who gave me confidence when I needed it

Published April 1991

ISBN 0-373-31147-8

THE THOROUGHLY COMPROMISED BRIDE

PROLOGUE

Summer 1807
Wiltshire, England

Miss Elizabeth Ashton had completed her second Season, a circumstance affording her nothing so much as heartfelt relief, very much as a child might feel when released from the schoolroom on a lovely spring day. To say that she had derived no pleasure from those two sojourns would be an untruth. She was not so unnatural. As much as any female did she enjoy the heady delights of a London Season. What she could *not* like were the multitude of musts and must-nots dictated to young females by the canons of propriety, many of which she need not regard when at home.

Had it been her choice alone, she would as lief have gone straight home after closing their London house, so eager was she to be at Wyndham Park again. But it was not her choice, and she could not be so selfish as to begrudge her papa and Aunt Emily the high treat of attending this house party, an end-of-Season assemblage hosted by their good

friends, Lord and Lady Langley. So she had, per-
force, been obliged to tarry here, kicking her heels
for the length of a sennight, and heartily bored by a
houseful of guests, none of whom had the least thing
in common with her. Yet her penance would soon be
at an end: they travelled to Wyndham on the mor-
row.

She had retired quite early, sensibly planning on a
long night of rest, but the excessive heat and her impatience to be gone had made sleep impossible. It
was very late, and turning from the window to the
rumpled, uninviting bed, she paused thoughtfully,
then, nodding her head decisively, slipped into her
dressing gown and stepped to the door. She turned
the knob carefully, opened the door and waited, listening. All was perfectly quiet, as it had been for at
least an hour. The rest of the house was fast asleep.

Leaving her room, she hurried along the corridor
and down the stairs to the library, where she opened
the French doors and slipped out onto the terrace. It
felt much cooler here and, she thought, well worth
this clandestine, nocturnal adventure. What would
be her aunt's reaction, were she to discover this in-
discretion, Elizabeth could well imagine: nothing less
than horrified shock, she was sure, which was quite
absurd, after all. What could possibly happen to her
here, she wondered, on a private estate belonging to
friends? She was as safe as if she were at home. Papa,

she knew, would think it a great joke and enjoy a good laugh over it.

She had been picking her way along the white gravel path which led through the garden, and soon came to a small summer house set back some distance from the house. It was a place that had proved to be a welcome retreat more than once since her arrival at Langley Hall, and stepping up to it now, she peered into the open doorway. It was pitch-black inside, and suddenly feeling a tiny thrill of unease, she turned to retrace her footsteps. Before she was able to take her first step, however, her arm was seized in a viselike grip, and she was pulled unceremoniously into the summer house. Fear and shock rendered her speechless.

A husky male voice murmured, "I was beginning to think you would not come."

Stunned into immobility and muteness, she was crushed in a strong embrace, her mouth covered in a harsh, demanding kiss, and for the first time in her life, Elizabeth feared she might faint.

After what seemed an eternity, her unknown assailant lifted his head, but as she opened her mouth to protest, it was again captured by his. This time his kiss was gentler and more sensuous, but she fought wildly upon feeling his tongue enter her mouth through her parted lips. Her efforts were of short duration. As a strange warmth spread through her body, making her knees feel weak, she stopped struggling against him, and her arms slid up to his shoulders. She was vaguely conscious of wondering how something which should be repugnant to her could feel so pleasant. However, all thought ceased after that, and Elizabeth's body took on a will of its own, responding to sensation after exquisite sensation as his tongue made a leisurely exploration of the sensitive interior of her mouth, and his knowing hands slowly tantalized her body.

With his mouth still on hers, he lifted her in his arms, carried her across the room to the chaise and laid her down. She lay there languorously, wondering why he was no longer touching her, but gradually came to her senses. Good God! What was she about? Was she waiting for him to attack her again? She sat up abruptly and said, "Please, you mustn't do this. It's a terrible mistake!"

The same husky voice she had heard before replied, "My dear, spare me your play-acting. Coyness really does not become you, and we both know you are no innocent. You've teased me long enough. Now the time has come to make good on all your promises."

As he spoke, he gently pushed her back and slid down beside her, half covering her body with his own. She raised her hand to push him away, gasping as she touched his bare chest, but again his mouth found hers. At the same time, his hand cupped her breast, his thumb rubbing softly across its peak, and she moaned as another incredible wave of pleasure swept through her body. When his lips moved to her throat and trailed lower to her breast, she was lost.

Later he softly kissed her eyelids, her nose and her mouth, and lightly caressing her shoulder, he murmured, "Ah, dearest, forgive me. I thought you were...someone else. Only tell me who you are and I'll make it up to you, I swear it!"

But Elizabeth, overwhelmed by what had happened, could only think of escape. Rolling away from him, she rose swiftly and ran from the summer house, straightening her nightclothes as she raced along the path to the house. When she had gained her room and locked the door, she began pacing from one side of the room to the other, trying to bring order to her chaotic thoughts and emotions.

How could such a thing have happened to her? How could she have enjoyed it so? With a blush of shame, she admitted that she had found pleasure in most of it. And in spite of the shame, the memory of those kisses, those caresses and all that had followed kept returning, unbidden, to cause a milder wave of that indescribable feeling to spread throughout her body.

Gradually she became calmer, and at last she sat on the edge of the bed asking herself what she must do. The answer came instantly: nothing. She must put this whole episode out of her mind as best she could, and go on as if nothing had occurred. No one must ever know of it and, after all, since she had no real wish to marry, it hardly mattered that, now, no man would want her for his wife.

Shortly after first light, having bade Lord and Lady Langley goodbye the evening before, Elizabeth, with her father and aunt, climbed into their carriage, and the coachman turned it towards home.

CHAPTER ONE

Winter 1814
Bath, England

IN THE MORNING ROOM of their house in Upper Camden Place, Aunt Emily and Elizabeth sat on opposite sides of the fireplace. The only sounds to be heard in the room were the crackling of the fire and an occasional exclamation from the elder of the two—a tiny, rounded birdlike woman—as she read the much crossed and recrossed letter in her lap. A smile played at the corners of Elizabeth's mouth upon hearing these small cries and utterances, but her remarkable grey eyes remained fixed upon her book.

Presently Aunt Emily looked up at her niece, her bright brown eyes alight with excitement, her letter fluttering in a little plump hand.

"Oh, my dear, you will never guess! Such diverting news!" she cried. "Lady Langley is coming to Bath!"

As always, the mention of Lady Langley's name produced a sudden fluttering sensation in Elizabeth's chest which she refused to acknowledge, and closing her book, she queried lightly, "Yes? And to what do we owe this treat?"

Her aunt smiled triumphantly. "Melanie is making her come-out!" This was said with an air of one making a momentous pronouncement. Then she frowned. "Though why Margaret should wish her to make her come-out in Bath is quite beyond me. It seems a very nip-faring way of doing the thing!"

"Melanie is Lady Langley's daughter, is she not? I expect she wishes the girl to try her wings here before making her London come-out. And I believe, my dear, that you mean to say nip-farthing."

"Yes, that's what I said. Well! It stands to reason that no one of any consequence would do anything so palfrey as to bring a girl out in Bath!"

"You mean paltry, Aunt. A palfrey is a horse," Elizabeth said automatically.

"What on earth has a horse to do with anything? Really, my love, you're not paying attention."

"I'm so sorry," her niece apologized in an unsteady voice. "When do they arrive?"

"Well, I'm not quite sure. Her letter is rather vagrant on that point."

Long familiarity with this small idiosyncrasy of her aunt's speech had rendered Elizabeth, for the most part, immune to it, but there were times when it became so pronounced that she could not resist quizzing Emily about it, and she said, "Is it erratic, my love? How very annoying!"

Her aunt stared at her. "Really, Elizabeth! Have you any idea how very difficult it is at times to have a conversation with you? I've spoken to you on that head before, my dear, and I wish you will pay attention, and keep to the subjective! There is nothing erotic about any of this!"

"Yes," replied her niece humbly. "I shall try to do better."

"Yes, well, as I was saying, it is not clear when they mean to arrive. However, they have taken a house in Laura Place, and there is nothing cheese-paving about that!"

"No, indeed!" agreed Elizabeth, controlling her countenance admirably.

"That is not to say, however, that they would not have done better to have taken a resonance here in Upper Camden Place."

"Oh, certainly! A resonance, er, residence here would have been much more the thing."

"However," her aunt declared, handsomely ignoring her slip, "that is neither here nor there!" She paused thoughtfully. "Where were we?"

"Lady Langley and Melanie are coming to Bath," supplied her niece.

"To be sure! They are coming for the winter, and I cannot help but think that it will do you a world of good, my love. To be seeing new faces and getting about more is just what you need. For you know, my dear, you have been entirely too redusive this past year, what with losing Sir Jonathan and Wyndham, too. But there! We shan't speak of those things.''

For just an instant, pain showed in Elizabeth's eyes. "No, pray, let us not. Though it's true that Papa's death was not expected, I always knew of the entailment, and that Wyndham would pass to Cousin Bertram when he was gone. I'm quite reconciled to it, you know, and quite happy with our own little home here.''

"Little home" was hardly an apt description of their elegant house in one of the most exclusive areas of Bath, but Emily allowed it to pass and with a far-away look in her eyes, she sighed. "It has been such a long time since I have seen Margaret. So odd how time seems to slip away from one, is it not?''

"Has it been so long?''

"Oh, yes. These six years and more. Do you know, the last time was at Langley Hall at the end of your last Season.''

Elizabeth automatically threw up a mental barrier against any memories associated with Langley Hall and fixed her attention upon the direction she knew the conversation was taking. A frown marred her brow. "Aunt Emily, do not, pray, begin teasing upon that subject again!''

If Elizabeth's expression did not warn her aunt to hold her tongue, her tone of voice should have, but

Emily foolishly ignored both and said earnestly, "My dearest, I know how you dislike my saying so—but, indeed, how will you ever achieve a respectable marriage if you will not go to London, or anywhere else for that matter? If you could but look with just a trifle more favour upon Lord Braxton . . . but if you cannot . . ."

"I not only cannot look with favour upon him, it is all I can do to be civil to the man!"

"Yes, my dear, and I hope you know that I would never, never . . . However, if we *could* but go to London for the Season . . ."

"Enough! Will you never learn? How many times must I tell you that I haven't the slightest wish to marry?"

"But, Elizabeth, you cannot know what you are saying! *Every* female must wish to wed! The life of a single female is not an ideal one—not that I am unhappy, I do assure you—but, indeed, it cannot compare with the protection and consequence offered by marriage!"

Elizabeth's eyes flashed dangerously. "No, let us not pick this bone again! It's been picked clean!" She opened her book, signalling her intention to end the conversation.

How she hated it when they got into such discussions. Why could her aunt not accept her decision to remain unmarried? And—oh Lord!—why must she be reminded of that one wretched event in her life?

The talk of marriage, combined with Lady Langley's proposed visit, was making it very difficult to keep unwanted memories at bay.

Emily Godwin gazed at her niece and sighed. From the tip of her golden head to the bottom of her dainty feet the girl was an incomparable. A nonpareil she had been called, but of course, that had been more than six years ago. Six years in which she had buried herself in the country with no man's company but her father's, and now here in Bath. Oh, it was so exasperating! And though one shouldn't think ill of the dead, Sir Jonathan had been a selfish care-for-nobody. He should have made a push to see Elizabeth married.

Still, it was not too late. She would defy anyone to deny that Elizabeth was as lovely, or even lovelier now, with maturity. If only she weren't so obstinate! It was beyond anything that the girl should behave as though she were past praying for. When she thought of the excellent matches Elizabeth had refused during her two Seasons, she could have wept with vexation! Then to have declined to go for another Season during the succeeding years was really too bad of her!

Miss Godwin sighed loudly again, and Elizabeth, calmer now, as well as feeling a trifle remorseful for having flown out at Emily, laid her book aside and gave her aunt a look of exasperated amusement.

"Come, Aunt Emily, let's cry peace. I'm sorry to have spoken so sharply to you. Do, pray, forgive me," she begged, and somewhat spoiled the effect of this pretty apology by adding, "but you know, you did provoke me!"

"But really, my dear, what else can you expect when you are determined to persist in this foolish notion of remaining a spinster? What will people say?"

"Good God! I care nothing for that!" said Elizabeth, laughing suddenly. "I suppose they will say that I am just another Bath Quiz. I may even become an eccentric recluse, and carry a cane with which I shall beat off all callers. Yes, and I shall wear nothing but black, and—"

"You would not!" cried her aunt in horrified accents.

"Well, perhaps not."

"You are pleased to joke about it, but it is not a laughing matter! And I know very well where to lay the blame! Your father was entirely at fault!"

"Nonsense! Papa had nothing to do with my decision not to marry."

"Indeed he did, and though you will not wish to hear it, I must say that had he not treated you more like a son than a daughter, you would not now be so shockingly independent!"

"What has that to say to anything? I promise you, it is not for that reason I wish to remain single."

"Then it is all those romances you have read that have done the mischief! They have given you the very odd notion that you cannot marry where you do not love. And, indeed, nothing could be further from the truth! I daresay if I put my mind to it, I might think of a dozen cases where love did not enter into the matter at all, and really, such couples manage to rub along together quite tolerably!"

"As happy as grigs, in fact, but be that as it may, I no longer look for love, and I do not intend to marry!"

"But, Elizabeth . . ."

"Oh, the devil! I do not wish to speak of this any longer!"

"I wish you would not use that language, my dear. Not that I blame *you*. Had your father not taught you to speak so— Yes!—and then laughed when you did—but, you should not—"

Miss Godwin was interrupted by Wiggons, their elderly butler, who entered the room to announce that Lord Braxton had arrived to pay them a morning call, and he enquired regally, "Are you at home to visitors, miss?"

Elizabeth's relief at this interruption of what was, to her a most distasteful discussion, was offset by irritation upon hearing Lord Braxton's name, but after a brief hesitation, she answered pleasantly enough, "Why, of course, Wiggons. You may show him up."

The man who entered the room a short time later was of stocky build and medium height. He was somewhere between thirty and forty years of age, with sandy-coloured, thinning hair, slightly protuberant eyes of a faded blue, and rather heavy features. He was dressed with propriety, but not modishly, for the points of his shirt collar rose no higher than his jawline, his neckcloth, while neatly tied, was not remarkable, and his coat, though undoubtedly well made, fitted too loosely to be entirely fashionable.

Lord Braxton considered himself to be the region's greatest matrimonial catch, but never, until the advent of Elizabeth, had he met a female whom he thought worthy of becoming his wife.

He was obviously in no doubt of his welcome, and going immediately to Emily, he bowed over her hand and said, "Ah, Miss Godwin, you become prettier each time I see you. If I am not careful, I shall be losing you to another beau!"

Emily tittered bashfully. "Oh, my lord, do stop fanning me! You are such a rogue!"

"Now, dear lady, you must know that I was not funning you. It is always a delight to see you."

"And I you, my lord," she said coyly.

These pleasantries out of the way, he judged it permissible to turn to Elizabeth, and carrying her hand to his lips, he bestowed an unwelcome kiss upon it, saying fervently, "My dear Miss Ashton! I need not tell you, I feel sure, what happiness it gives me to see you.''

Elizabeth forced a smile as she retrieved her hand. ''How good of you to call, sir.''

''Yes,'' he agreed, ''but not having seen you for the length of a whole day, my dear, I could not stay away. You will allow me, I know, to tell you that you are more lovely each time I see you.''

''Thank you,'' she said coolly, and to forestall any more of his fulsome compliments, she asked quickly, ''How is your mother, Lord Braxton?''

Lady Braxton, who lived with her son, was a robust woman who thrived on infirmity, going from one alarming malady to another.

''I am very much afraid that she is not at all well,'' said Lord Braxton somberly, and he launched into a lengthy description of his mother's most recent sufferings.

Nothing could have been more delightfully interesting to Emily, and she spent some time discussing a variety of cures and remedies with his lordship.

With that topic finally exhausted, he entertained them with the newest on-dits from Town, and then favoured them with a detailed account of his latest improvements to his estate. Aunt Emily flattered and encouraged him throughout all this, while Elizabeth endured it stoically. By the end of the requisite half hour, when he stood to take his leave of them, she felt sure that had she been forced to listen for another moment to his prosing, she must have been provoked into screaming.

"I shall call again tomorrow," he promised them, "for I know you will wish to hear how my mother goes on."

"Oh, yes! We certainly shall!" Emily assured him. "You must call and tell us everything. Poor lady, how she does suffer!"

"Yes," he agreed, "and bears it so well."

Miss Godwin shook her head in wonderment. "It is truly amusing!"

Elizabeth choked. "Amazing, Aunt."

"Yes, I knew you would think so, too."

Lord Braxton now gave an arch smile and said, "I had almost forgot! Among my reasons for calling was a wish to learn if I shall have the pleasure of seeing you dear ladies at the concert this evening."

"How delightful that would be!" Emily cried enthusiastically.

"I am not at all sure that I feel up to going out this evening, Aunt. Let us discuss it later," Elizabeth said hastily.

"My dear Miss Ashton, I should be most distressed to hear that you are not feeling quite the thing," Lord Braxton told her. "I do hope your indisposition will not keep you from the concert. I shall look for you there and shall be quite disappointed if I do not see you."

At that moment, Wiggons appeared to announce the arrival of Mr. Charles Carlyle. The name was unfamiliar to Elizabeth, and she looked questioningly at her aunt. But before she could ask the question that hovered on her lips, their guest had entered the room.

Elizabeth turned, and her breath caught in her throat as she found herself gazing at the most handsome man she had ever beheld.

CHAPTER TWO

CONSIDERABLY TALLER than the average, Charles Carlyle paused in the doorway of the morning room with an air of polite boredom, his glance slowly taking in the room and its occupants, and at last coming to rest on Elizabeth.

He was dressed in tight-fitting breeches and highly polished topboots, his neckcloth was arranged to a nicety, and his coat of Bath superfine was exquisitely fashioned and fitted him like a glove. Yet no sartorial fussiness marred the elegance of his appearance.

His black hair was brushed into the Brutus style and one unruly lock fell over his forehead, softening the otherwise austere visage with its slightly aquiline nose, high cheekbones, square jawline and finely chiselled lips. All this Elizabeth saw before his intensely deep, blue eyes found and held hers irresistibly. For the space of several heartbeats they stood thus, until one of his dark brows arched questioningly, and his eyes narrowed in amusement.

Brought abruptly back to an awareness of her surroundings, Elizabeth felt her cheeks suffuse with colour, and she could only be thankful when his attention was drawn from her by Aunt Emily, who exclaimed, "Oh, Charles! What a very pleasant surprise! But does this mean that Margaret is here in Bath? I had not expected it so soon."

The smile that Charles directed at Emily transformed his face, banishing all trace of arrogance and boredom, and bowing to her, he replied, "Why, yes ma'am, we arrived yesterday evening. My sister has charged me with delivering a message to you. She is all at sixes and sevens today getting settled in, but wishes me to tell you that she hopes to have all put to rights by tomorrow, and will call on you in the morning."

"So kind," breathed Emily. "I shall so look forward to seeing her again. But where are my manners? Charles, you are equated with my niece, of course."

Charles appeared startled, and Elizabeth's eyes danced as she interposed, "You mean acquainted, Aunt Emily."

"Yes, dear, that is what I said."

Charles looked at Elizabeth with both amusement and appreciation before answering Emily. "No, ma'am, I've not had that pleasure."

Emily frowned in puzzlement, saying, "No? I made sure...well, no matter. Elizabeth, this is Lady Langley's brother, Charles Carlyle. Charles, my niece, Elizabeth Ashton."

By this time Elizabeth had recovered sufficient composure to extend her hand to him, and with a coolly polite smile, said, "Mr. Carlyle. How do you do?"

He raised her hand slowly to his lips, his eyes never leaving hers and murmured, "Very well indeed, Miss Ashton. I had no idea, when I agreed to deliver Margaret safely to Bath, that it would prove to be such an interesting place."

It was Elizabeth's turn to raise an eyebrow as she said, "No doubt you are referring to the Pump Room, the Assembly Rooms and our many other attractions."

"Just so! Especially the 'other attractions.' "

The corners of her mouth twitched in response to his wicked grin, but before she could make a suitable retort, a loud throat-clearing caused three pairs of startled eyes to swing round to the forgotten Lord Braxton, who was fairly quivering with indignation at having been ignored for so long.

"Oh, my dear Lord Braxton," gasped Emily, "we have been indulging in the most inexcludible behaviour! Pray, forgive us and allow me to make Mr. Carlyle known to you."

Charles gazed at Emily in fascination.

Lord Braxton, his countenance stiffened with disapproval, said, "I am acquainted with Mr. Carlyle, and you will not object, I know, Miss Godwin, when I say that he is *not* a fit acquaintance for a delicately nurtured female such as Miss Ashton. It would be remiss of me were I not to inform you of this, and, indeed, a shirking of my duty as your friend." He glared at Charles, who merely smiled sardonically as though he were enjoying the whole situation immensely.

Elizabeth's eyes flashed with anger. "Lord Braxton, you go too far! When I wish your advice as to whom I may be acquainted with, I shall tell you! But you were just leaving, were you not? We mustn't detain you!"

As a distressed Aunt Emily tried to smooth Lord Braxton's ruffled feathers, Charles whispered, "Good girl!" into Elizabeth's ear, and so inordinately pleased was she at this approbation that she had difficulty maintaining the quelling stare with which she was regarding Lord Braxton.

His lordship very obviously had no wish to leave while Charles remained, but was unable to think of an appropriate excuse for staying. He said only, "Well, well, we shall speak of this another time when you are feeling more yourself. I shall look for you, dear ladies, this evening at the concert." With that, he finally took his leave.

While Emily accompanied him to the door of the room, still talking soothingly, Elizabeth turned to Charles with laughter in her eyes and said in a low voice, "You must not encourage me in being rude to a guest."

"If giving that pompous toad a set-down he richly deserves is being rude, then I certainly shall encourage you! For that matter, why do you encourage him to dangle after you?"

"No, no! I don't! It's Aunt Emily who does that! But it takes very little to encourage him, I fear, for he has an excessively high regard for himself."

"Give him a damper and send him to rout," he advised her.

"Do you think I have not tried? I assure you I have, but the man is impervious to insults and rejections alike. Add to that the fact that he cannot bring himself to imagine that any female would not be thrown into transports by his attentions, and the situation becomes impossible."

"Would you like me to discourage him?" Charles laughed. "I could, you know."

"Good heavens! I'm afraid to ask how you might do it," she said, her eyes twinkling.

He smiled. "Oh, nothing too drastic—merely one of my famous set-downs. However, let's not waste our time speaking of him. Tell me, instead, does your aunt always exhibit that peculiar manner of speech?"

She gave another gurgle of laughter. "Not always, but frequently. Especially when she is excited or overset, which is most of the time!"

"But what an endless source of amusement for you," he said, his eyes crinkling with laughter.

"Yes," she agreed. "But she is really a dear, and I don't know how I should go on without her."

"Lends you countenance, in fact, does she?"

"Exactly so!"

Before he could reply to this, Aunt Emily returned from seeing Lord Braxton out, and they all sat down as she said, "What a pity that Lord Langley could not come with Margaret—not that I am not excessively happy to see you, Charles—but I do hope that he is not indisposed!"

"Oh, as to that, I believe him to be as hale and hearty as ever. He always is, you know," Charles replied.

"Oh! Then I collect it is pressing estate business that prevents his being with us."

Charles laughed. "My dear lady, he never troubles himself with such matters. He has an excellent agent to handle all that for him. No! The only circumstance to prevent his being with us, I fear, is an excessive dislike of Bath, and a sad disinclination to do anything which might interfere with his own pleasures!"

"Oh!" said Emily, disconcerted by such frankness.

"You will have us believe, sir, that you hold an aversion to your brother-in-law," Elizabeth remarked.

"No, no!" he assured her. "I like him quite well. He is a most agreeable fellow."

"Well, it was kind of you to stand in for him," she said.

"Not at all!" he replied. "I could wish to leave you with that happy impression of me, but in the interest of honesty, I must confess that it was not kindness that induced me to give escort to my sister and niece. Margaret bullied me into it!"

Elizabeth smiled. "I find it hard to believe that you can be bullied."

"How perceptive of you, Miss Ashton. In general, you are quite right, but when you know my sister better, you will see how it came about."

"Oh!" cried Emily. "I am very sure that Margaret would not wish to force upon you anything which you might not like! I am persuaded that you are quizzing us!"

"Just so, ma'am," he answered her gravely, but with a tell-tale quiver at the corner of his mouth.

Such subtleties were lost on Emily, and happy to have been reassured on that point, she asked, "Will you be making a long stay in Bath, Mr. Carlyle?"

"I had not planned on doing so," he replied, and glancing at Elizabeth he continued, "However, now that I am here, it seems a shame not to stay... and enjoy all its attractions."

Elizabeth was furious to feel herself blushing, and was glad that the next few minutes were spent in nothing more than polite social conversation before Charles left them.

When he had gone, she asked her aunt, "Why did you not tell me that Lady Langley's brother would be with her?"

"Oh, did I not?"

"No, my dear, you did not." Elizabeth paused for a moment, then asked, "Do you know him well?"

"Well, no, for he is much younger than Margaret, and was away at school for much of the time when we were growing up."

"He seems a most interesting man," Elizabeth remarked casually.

"Yes," said Emily uncertainly, and then added in a worried tone of voice, "Do you suppose that Lord Braxton may be right about him? I *have* heard...but nothing disreputable. Oh, Elizabeth, it would be too mortifying to find that I have introduced you to a...a..."

"A loose screw?" supplied Elizabeth mischievously.

Emily's eyes rounded in shock. "No, no! Oh, you mustn't say such things! But, indeed, it would be very wrong in me to countenance an acquaintance between you and a...a man of unsalivary reputation!"

Elizabeth, who had not, since the death of her father, enjoyed anyone's company half so much, declared firmly, "Nonsense! I wish you will tell me how you might have avoided introducing us, and I saw nothing in him to take exception to. He seemed the perfect gentleman." She quickly suppressed a twinge of conscience at having twisted the truth a little before adding, "At any rate, he is Lady Langley's brother, so we cannot very well cut him. It wouldn't be at all the thing to do! Besides which, I don't imagine that he'll remain here for long. A man such as he must find our small entertainments very dull stuff indeed.''

She knew a feeling of disappointment at this thought, but her aunt appeared most relieved, and agreed happily, "Oh, yes. I feel sure you are right!" And, reaching for her tambour frame, she dismissed Mr. Charles Carlyle from her mind, a feat Elizabeth found much more difficult to accomplish.

When, later, the subject of the concert was again brought up, Elizabeth consented to go, not even asking herself why it now seemed so desirable. However, an evening that should have been at least mildly enjoyable turned out to be strangely flat. All the while she listened to the music and made polite conversation, her eyes sought a tall, masculine figure with broad shoulders and a pair of keen, laughing blue eyes. It was to no avail, for he did not appear.

On the return journey to Upper Camden Place, where she and Aunt Emily were escorted by Lord Braxton, Elizabeth was unusually quiet, merely giving the briefest of answers when any remark was addressed to her. She was feeling a vague sense of dissatisfaction, and a lowering of spirits which she was at a loss to understand. Upon arriving home, she immediately excused herself and retired to her bedchamber.

She had planned and ordered her life exactly to her liking, never once regretting any of it. Before ever being launched among the ton, she had known that she would never marry where there was no love, and though she had received several very flattering offers, she had felt nothing more than mild liking for the men who had made them. So she had already considered the very real possibility that she might live out her life as a single woman even before that fateful house party, and had accepted that prospect with equanimity. Afterwards, of course, the matter was no longer one of choice, but of necessity, and still she had not been at all dismayed by it. Over the years she had seen enough marriages to feel that she was not missing anything. Few, if any, appeared happy enough to warrant relinquishing all control of oneself to some man. Fortunately, being comfortably circumstanced, she could afford to carve out a life of her own design. So why a future that had appeared entirely satisfactory and comfortable—even desirable—should now suddenly look rather bleak and dull was beyond her ability to fathom.

By this time she was out of reason cross with herself for falling prey to this fit of the dismals, and at last, climbing into bed, she muttered, "Oh, the devil take it all!" And after a moment, she added, "And Charles Carlyle, too!"

She was attaching entirely too much importance to the man, she decided, and deliberately turned her thoughts to other matters until, at last, she fell asleep.

CHAPTER THREE

AWAKENING THE NEXT MORNING with the sun shining in her window, and feeling marvellously refreshed and cheerful, Elizabeth did not question the cause of her good spirits but was merely thankful that her mood had lifted, and after a leisurely breakfast, she went to change into clothing more suitable for the out-of-doors.

She entered the morning room a short time later, pulling on her gloves. She was clad in a walking dress of light blue; a velvet pelisse of darker blue, trimmed in fur, covered it; and a matching velvet bonnet with ostrich-plume trim, its high poke lined with gathered silk, was tied under one ear. She looked entirely charming.

As she stepped lightly across the room to her aunt, Emily looked up from her stitching in surprise, exclaiming, "But you cannot be going out! Have you forgot? Margaret is coming this morning."

Elizabeth leaned down to kiss her cheek. "No, dear, I have not forgot, and, indeed, I am going out," she replied. "Lady Langley will be here all winter, and I will have any number of opportunities to visit with her, but I am persuaded that after six years the two of you will have all manner of things to talk over. You will enjoy a comfortable coze without me here to interfere.''

"Oh, no! How can you think you would be interfering?" Emily protested.

Smiling and shaking her head, Elizabeth raised her hand to stop the other's objections. "No, don't try to change my mind. It's quite made up. I am going to do some shopping and then look in at the Pump Room. Have you any errands for me while I am out?"

Emily capitulated. "No, dear, but you are not going alone, are you?"

Throwing both hands up in mock horror, Elizabeth cried, "Good heavens! I wouldn't dream of it! I shall take Jennings with me."

With a small sniff, her aunt complained, "It's all very well for you to laugh, but you know that you have not enough respect for the proprieties!"

"Yes, I know, best of aunts; I am a sad trial to you, am I not?" And with that, Elizabeth made her exit, and was soon leaving the house, properly accompanied by her maid.

She set a brisk pace until they reached Milsom Street, where she visited several shops, purchasing new gloves, stockings, some ribbon and a delectable bonnet which she had no need of, but which she could not resist. After leaving the last shop, she informed Jennings pleasantly but firmly that she would no longer need her, and instructed her to carry the packages home. Jennings, who had been with her mistress since her emergence from the schoolroom, was reluctant to leave her unattended but knew better than to waste breath in argument. So with a loud sniff of disapproval, and saying only, "Yes, Miss Elizabeth," she turned, and made her way back to Upper Camden Place alone, while Elizabeth proceeded to Stall Street and the Pump Room.

Surveying the room rapidly, she soon spied her friend, Mrs. Gilbert, sitting at the far end with several other ladies, and Elizabeth began threading her way through the various groups crowding the room, stopping frequently to exchange greetings with those residents who were well known to her. She was still some distance from Mrs. Gilbert when a hand on her elbow caused her to look up quickly, a rebuke on her lips, only to draw a sharp breath as Charles Carlyle smiled down on her warmly. She lowered her eyes swiftly, hoping to hide the unexpected rush of joy she felt upon seeing him. "Damnation!" she muttered under her breath. Was she destined to gasp and blush like a schoolgirl each time she met him? What a silly wet-goose she was!

Leaning towards her with laughter in his eyes, he said, "I know how very eager you are to join your friends, but pray stay with me for a while." Placing her hand on his arm, he began to stroll with her towards the other end of the room.

Glancing up at him teasingly, she enquired, "What brings you to our famous gathering place? Have you come to drink the waters, sir?"

"Good God, no! I came in the hope of seeing you."

Surprised, she declared, "What a bouncer! You couldn't possibly have known that I would be here this morning."

"True, but I was prepared to haunt the place until you did appear, however long it took."

"Now that's doing it much too brown! You must know that you have only to call in Upper Camden Place to see me, if that is your object."

"Do you doubt it? I assure you, it is an object with me to see you as often as I may. But in Upper Camden Place I must always share you with your aunt."

Flustered, she could think of no answer to this, but he continued, "By the way, did you know that you sometimes use language and terms that one hardly expects from a gently nurtured female? Never tell me that your aunt taught you that manner of speaking!"

She could not help laughing. "Oh, dear! If you knew how funny that is! But no, of course she did not. Papa taught me."

"Your papa taught you?" he asked in some surprise.

"Well, yes, I'm afraid he did. You see, Papa always wished for a son and heir, but when Mama died—while I was still a baby—he decided to make the best of things, and treated me more like a son than a daughter."

"Good God!" he ejaculated. "Was he blind?"

"No, of course not! And I did have Aunt Emily and Nurse Sedgewick to teach me how I should go on as a female, but the thing is that Papa never watched his tongue when I was about or reprimanded me when I picked up some of his words and expressions. Indeed, he thought it excessively amusing and always laughed. And you must know, those habits can be the very devil to break. Oh! I beg your pardon! What must you think of me!"

He laughed. "Yes, you show a sad want of conduct, my girl!"

"I promise you, I shall try much harder to be careful in the future."

"Well, I hope you are not too successful," he said, his eyes still alight with amusement, "for a find it extremely diverting. Tell me, what other interesting habits did your papa teach you?"

"Well, I dislike people who brag excessively, but I must own that I am a bruising rider, and no mean whipster, either. But I fear Papa was quite disappointed at my lack of aptitude in all matters to do with sports, and try as I would, I could *not* develop a taste for port!"

He gave a shout of laughter, drawing the curious stares of those about them, and lowering his voice, he said, "You delightful girl! What will you say next?"

With a rueful grin she answered, "Well, there is no telling, so pray, do not egg me on!"

He merely chuckled, and they continued slowly round the room in silence for several minutes until he drew her to an abrupt halt. Following his frowning gaze, she saw Lord Braxton bearing down upon them with determination writ clearly on his face.

"Ah, fair lady," he cried effusively, availing himself of her free hand. "Seeing your lovely face this morning has brightened my day immeasurably!"

"Good morning, my lord," said Elizabeth, pulling her hand from his.

Charles acknowledged his presence with a slight nod, and murmured, "Braxton."

Lord Braxton directed a stare replete with loathing at Charles before turning once more to Elizabeth. "Miss Ashton, I am sure you will understand me, and be in perfect agreement when I say that I believe it would be best if I were to return you to your aunt." He cast his eyes about the room as he asked, "But where is Miss Godwin? I do not see her anywhere."

Elizabeth's chin came up obstinately as she informed him, "My aunt is at home, sir. I came alone today."

"What?" he responded, his eyes swinging back to her face. They seemed very nearly ready to pop from his head, and so absurd an appearance did he present that she quickly averted her face in order not to succumb to the bubble of laughter that threatened to escape her throat. Unfortunately, her stricken eyes met Mr. Carlyle's, and they both burst into laughter.

His lordship drew himself up stiffly, and waited, a study in injured dignity, until Elizabeth and Charles managed to regain their composure.

As soon as she was able, Elizabeth gasped, "Oh, pray forgive us, my lord. It was only... I mean..."

"Well!" pronounced Lord Braxton severely. "I cannot like this tendency towards levity in you, Miss Ashton. It is to be hoped most devoutly that with the proper influence— But this is neither the time nor the place for that. I will speak to you of that at another time. Come, my dear, I shall see you home."

Charles Carlyle looked down at him from hooded eyes, a disdainful smile curling his lips. "Sorry, Braxton, but I've already offered to see the lady home. No, don't eat me! I know you wish me to the devil, but I don't intend to oblige you just now."

"Sir, I find your language offensive!" his antagonist told him in outraged tones. "I would remind you that there is a lady present!"

"I doubt the lady finds my language as offensive as your behaviour. You are making a cake of yourself, man. Worse than that, you are embarrassing Miss Ashton. Give over!''

"Not only are you offensive, Mr. Carlyle, but you are insulting as well, and I shall not stand for your insults!''

"Is that a challenge, Braxton? Or are you merely offering to mill me down?"

Never before had Lord Braxton been so tempted to challenge a man to a duel, but a strong sense of self-preservation prevented it. However, shaking with emotion, his face alarmingly red, and his mouth working, he had to pause for a moment before he was able to gain enough control to say coldly, "I am sure Miss Ashton is deeply grateful for your offer, sir, but she will not wish to put you to any further trouble now that I am here."

He reached confidently for Elizabeth's arm, but she stepped back quickly, avoiding his grasp, and said, "No! You needn't bother, my lord. I have told Mr. Carlyle that I should be glad of his escort."

And with that, Elizabeth and Charles walked away, leaving Lord Braxton sputtering impotently.

When they had left the Pump Room, Elizabeth tried to school her expression into one of stern reproach, but laughter hovered at the edge of her voice as she said, "Oh, shameless! Now see what you have done! You've made a liar of me."

"I see what it is. You have a tendre for him."

"Oh, was anything ever more ridiculous?" she cried. "Well, you are fair and far out there! And if you think any such thing, you must have windmills in your head!"

He smiled at her but made no answer, and they walked on companionably until he suddenly asked, "Why do you come out unattended? Is this the custom now prevailing in this part of the country?"

"No, of course not, but it is not so necessary here as it would be in London, especially for me, since I am far past the age of needing a chaperon."

His eyes gleamed with amusement. "No! Are you? How well preserved you are, ma'am. But then I cannot help wondering how it comes about that a woman of such advanced age has never married."

Elizabeth gasped. "Really, sir! That can be no concern of yours."

"Possibly not. But why haven't you?"

"Good God! What an ill-mannered, uncivil man you are!"

"Do you think so? That seems a little harsh to me. But why have you never married?"

In exasperation, Elizabeth answered angrily, "Because I like my life very well as it is. And . . . and I have never wished to marry. And this is a most improper conversation for us to be having!"

"Yes, isn't it?" he agreed unabashedly.

"Well, if you know that, why do you persist in such impropriety?"

He looked at her with an inscrutable smile, but ignored her question, saying instead, "Do you know, I have the feeling that you are not being entirely honest with me. What other reason have you for not marrying? I cannot believe that you've received no offers."

"Certainly I have," she could not resist saying. "Three unexceptional ones in fact, and I refused them all."

"Hmm. I wonder why? Come, my dear, what do you have against marriage?"

"The devil!" she cried. "I do not intend to discuss this with you any further, sir! Suffice it to say that marriage holds no allure for me. And you are a fine one to talk!"

He burst out laughing. "Ah! There's my charmer. Shall I tease you until I learn your secret, my sweet?"

This was coming too close for comfort and, lips compressed, she disdained to answer, resorting to silence again, which neither attempted to break for some time, until finally she said, "I wish you would stop addressing me in that improper manner. I am neither your 'sweet,' nor your 'charmer.'"

"Now there I'm afraid I must differ with you. You must allow me to know what you are to me. However, if it will please you, I'll address you only as ma'am, or Miss Ashton when anyone else is about. When we are alone, it is a different matter."

"I suppose I should be glad of that much at least. Do you know you are really quite impossible?"

He squeezed her hand, laughing down at her, and she found it difficult not to smile back at him, difficult to remain angry with him. She could certainly see why he had the reputation of being a rake! He was impudent and a shocking flirt—and utterly irresistible. She knew that she ought to remonstrate with him more, ought to insist that he address her properly at all times. She also knew that she was allowing him to behave with far too much intimacy towards her. But she did enjoy his flirting, and as long as she realized that it was no more, it seemed harmless enough. Besides, if she did not let it drop, he would very likely say something even more outrageous!

He broke in on her thoughts then, saying, "Tell me, what do you do for entertainment here?"

Relieved at the change of topic, she answered, "Oh, we have any number of amusements to keep us entertained. At the New Assembly Rooms there are balls on Monday and Thursday evenings, and if you care for cards, there are two card rooms there. There are concerts every Wednesday evening, and I believe there are balls and entertainments at the Lower Rooms as well, though I've not been to them. In addition there are private balls and—"

"Stop!" he cried with a laugh. "I can see that your social life is quite hectic. You must be worn to a thread after a week of such frantic gaiety."

Unable to withhold an answering grin, she admitted, "It *is* a trifle dull at times," then quickly assured him, "but you needn't consider me an object deserving of your pity! I am seldom bored, and can always find something to hold my interest."

"My beautiful little pea-goose. Pity is *not* what I feel for you!"

She blinked at him, blushing rosily, but as they had by then arrived at her doorstep, she was not obliged to answer and said instead, "Thank you for walking with me, though it wasn't at all necessary."

"Much as it pains me to contradict you, my girl, there was every necessity. It really is not the thing for young females to go traipsing through town unattended."

In her haughtiest voice she replied, "Sir, I have told you before that I am long since past the age of having to worry that such things will damage my reputation."

"Oh, yes, an ape leader in fact!" he said, and touching her cheek lightly with one finger, a heart-stopping look of warmth in his eyes again, he turned and strode away.

CHAPTER FOUR

IN THE MEANTIME, Emily and Margaret had indeed enjoyed a comfortable coze. Over tea, they brought each other up to date on the particulars of their lives. It took little time to dispense with the previous six years: they had, after all, written to one another frequently, and conversation soon moved on to more current topics. Chief amongst these were gossip concerning mutual friends, the latest news from London and plans for the winter.

Lady Langley, a handsome, formidable-looking matron, finally asked, "Well, and how does Elizabeth do?"

Emily replied, "Oh, she does very well. She is the dearest girl!"

"Girl? Hardly that! She must have close on six-and-twenty years in her dish by now!"

"Well, yes—very nearly."

Shrewdly, her ladyship asked, "Do I detect a note of concern in your voice? Out with it, Emily. What's troubling you?"

"Oh, no, it's nothing—truly!"

Her friend snorted. "Don't try to flummery me! I know you too well." And after a hesitation, she asked, "Why hasn't she married?"

Emily sat forward in her chair. "Now, there you have put your finger on the very problem. Heaven knows that it isn't for lack of opportunity. Why, even now I am in daily explication of Lord Braxton's making her an offer." Then she added, her voice sinking with dejection, "But I would be astonished if she were to accept him."

"Why ever should she not? What is wrong with him?"

"Nothing in the world!" cried Emily bitterly. "Everything about him is just as it should be. Only she will say that she does not love him."

"Oh, love!" said Lady Langley wisely. "Well, I cannot have anything to say against that. Mine, after all, was a love match. However, there is still something to be said for arranged marriages. What a pity they have gone out of style!"

"Indeed, I have said so to Elizabeth often and often, but to no avail. And why she should wish to dwindle into an old maid is something I cannot understand, but so it is."

Nodding her head sympathetically, her friend replied, "Yes, I can comprehend your feelings exactly! Charles is just such another sad case, though the unmarried state is not, in the ordinary way, the tragedy for a male that it is for a female. Time out of mind I've told that ramshackle brother of mine to find himself a wife and set up his nursery. 'Twould be the making of him, I don't doubt, but he's frustrated my every effort at matchmaking.'' Laughing merrily, she continued, ''Do you know, at one time I even thought that he and Elizabeth would suit, and did my best to bring them together, but it came to nought.''

''Oh? I didn't know. Pray, when was that?''

''Why, six years ago when I had all of you for my house party. After commanding Charles to be there without fail, I had thought to have an entire sennight in which to promote the match, but the perverse creature only arrived on the last evening, and then only after Elizabeth had gone early to bed—so very provoking it was! I have always suspected that his only reason for appearing at all was to see Lady Sabina, and thank God *that* affair died aborning, for you know, her husband was not at all inclined to look the other way.''

Emily could only reply faintly, ''Oh, yes,'' for she was a much less sophisticated soul than Lady Langley, and easily shocked. In fact, two more unlikely confidantes would be hard to discover, but they had grown up as close neighbours, and friends they remained, in spite of their disparities.

There was a pause in the conversation, and Emily asked with a puzzled frown, ''But why did they never meet in London?''

"Elizabeth and Charles? That's easily explained. Like as not they never attended the same functions. He's had so many chits flung at his head by their predatory mamas that for years he's avoided each new crop like the plague."

Emily sighed for what might have been. "Oh, dear! What a pity! Elizabeth and Charles...I should like it above all things. But perhaps...I mean, is he not...? that is, I have heard..." and with face flaming, she finished in a strangled voice, "his reputation?"

This drew another peal of laughter from her friend, and she answered, "Oh, Lord, yes, he is a shocking reprobate! But what does that signify? He is still one of the most eligible partis anywhere in England, and depend upon it, my dear, there is no better husband than a reformed rake, and no better way to reform one than putting him in the way of the right female."

"But, Margaret, now that they *have* met, perhaps they may yet make a match of it."

"Not if they're left to themselves! I daresay they'd mismanage the affair miserably. However, you and I might contrive to bring the thing off, though I warn you, it will be no easy task. I don't depend upon his remaining with me above one or two more days. But we won't despair. I shall try, if I can, to devise a way to keep him longer."

"Oh, you will, I feel sure! As clever as you are!"

And the two conspirators smiled happily at each other just as Elizabeth, returning, came into the room.

If her heightened colour was remarked at all, it was attributed to the coldness of the weather, and after staring critically for a moment, Lady Langley declared, "Well, Elizabeth, I have never seen you in better looks."

"Thank you, ma'am. I need not ask how you do, for you look delightfully."

"Handsomely said, my dear."

Emily interrupted these civilities to say accusingly, "Oh, Elizabeth, never say you walked home alone! And do not think to pull the wolf over my eyes, for I saw Jennings return some time ago!"

"No, Aunt Emily. You need not rake me over the coals. Mr. Carlyle was kind enough to escort me home, and you'll be pleased to hear that he agrees with you completely, though I am surprised that *he* of all people should be such a champion of propriety!" In sudden realization, Elizabeth glanced at Lady Langley guiltily. "Forgive me, ma'am. I should not have said that."

Lady Langley laughed gaily. "Oh, you need not apologize, my dear. I know my brother only too well! And I must tell you that when it comes to the question of a lady's reputation, the most hardened rake can become an absolute prig."

Elizabeth refrained from commenting upon such hypocrisy, and after chatting for a few minutes, Lady Langley took her leave, plans having been made before her departure, for them to meet the following morning in the Pump Room.

UPON ENTERING the Pump Room the next day, Elizabeth and Emily found Lady Langley and Melanie already there, and wasted no time in taking them over to join Mrs. Gilbert. That lady was the proud mother of a young daughter, and the two girls, being nearly the same age, were soon chattering together in a lively manner that boded well for a blossoming friendship.

The women watched them for several minutes, the older three indulgently, and Elizabeth with amusement. But when the women began to converse, and the discourse turned to child-rearing, Elizabeth found her attention wandering. Excusing herself to go to Meyler and Sons Library, which conveniently adjoined the Pump Room, she hurried away, promising to return before they should be ready to leave.

In a very short time, she was contentedly browsing through the stacks of books, stopping now and then to read a few lines in the more promising of them. She was stretching for one on an upper shelf when a strong, masculine hand reached round her and lifted it down. Knowing instinctively who it would be before she turned her head, she glanced quickly up into Charles Carlyle's face. He was watching her with his peculiarly intent gaze, a lazy smile upon his lips, and she thought ruefully that at least she was becoming sufficiently inured to the sight of him to allow her some control over her response.

Perusing the title before handing the book to her, he said in a voice that was at once polite and oddly intimate, "Ah! A romance. So you are not entirely uninterested in that subject."

She lifted her chin a trifle defiantly. "On the contrary, sir," she replied coolly, "I find romances highly entertaining. I have, in fact, a great love of reading."

His expression remained perfectly sober, but a smile of pure amusement lit his eyes as he said, "Well, then, I think you will particularly like this one. I did."

She shot a surprised look at him. "Do you mean to say that you have read it?"

"Certainly I have. Does that surprise you?"

"Well, only because I had not thought that gentlemen read novels."

"I would venture to say that a great many gentlemen do, though they may stick at admitting it."

He waited until they had left the library, and were walking towards the Pump Room before saying, "Indeed, I am extremely fond of books—novels included. Many of them are old friends."

"Yes, that is exactly what I feel, and oh! how often they have rescued me from tedium." She had spoken with candid eagerness, but seeing his smile broaden, she added hurriedly, "Oh, dear, now you will be thinking that I find my life here a dead bore."

"No. I won't quiz you about it. We've already established the fact that life here is gay to dissipation." Then, becoming more serious, he continued, "Tell me, instead, of your life before coming to Bath—unless it would be too painful for you."

He knew something of her recent past from his sister, and his eyes, as well as the tone of his voice, held so much of kindness and understanding that she found herself talking of Wyndham as she had never been able to since its loss. She spoke of the grounds, the woods around it, the house itself; she told him how she missed her horses, and riding out each day; but most of all, how she missed the companionship of her father. Charles drew her out with interested questions, and when she was done, he in turn told her of his estate, Brentwood, in such vivid detail that she felt she knew it well.

They had arrived at the Pump Room long since, promenading as they talked, and now found seats near the others of their party. She saw by his expression that his mood had altered, and his eyes held a teasing light as he murmured, "Do you know, I have often found the observation of other people to be vastly entertaining and instructive. For instance, do you perceive that lady over there?''

Looking across the room, Elizabeth saw a female of such astounding appearance that she was startled into an involuntary giggle. Though short in height, in all other respects the lady was of truly astonishing proportions. She had a jolly face bounded by three magnificent chins, and a bonnet that was every bit as startling as the rest of her person, being adorned with four ostrich plumes, a profusion of fruit and two large rosettes. The rest of her attire was of an antiquated style, and no less awe-inspiring, for everything was of the brightest colours imaginable.

"Yes," said Charles gravely. "I see you have managed to pick her out of the crowd. I daresay you will be surprised to learn that the lady is a newcomer to our shores, a resident of a little-known foreign country where she is a member of the nobility...." He went on to weave a history so absurd that Elizabeth was shortly reduced to helpless laughter. She soon joined him in the game, and so an agreeable quarter hour was spent in choosing improbable heroes and heroines for their tales.

This growing intimacy was observed with amiable complacence by their respective relatives, and with wonder by Mrs. Gilbert, until the girls returned from walking round the room. They were bubbling over with excitement and plans for their own amusement.

"Oh, Mama!" cried Melanie. "Only think! Mr. Graham and Mr. Kirby, who are friends of Lucinda's, wish to form a party to ride up to Lansdown, and they have been so kind as to invite me to join them. Only say that I may, please?"

"Well, but my dear," replied her mother, "I cannot like the scheme if there are only you young people going. And you cannot expect me to spend even so short a time in the saddle. I do not remember when I was last on a horse!"

Mrs. Gilbert concurred with these sentiments, and both girls' faces fell in disappointment, but were quickly wreathed in smiles again as Charles said, "There could be no objection if Miss Ashton and I rode out with them."

The girls were thrilled at this suggestion, and Charles looked to Elizabeth for approval. She would not have denied him for the world, for to be riding again would be, of all things, most agreeable to her. But she had no sooner given her smiling assent than she exclaimed in dismay, "Oh, but I have no horse! You see, I sold mine when we removed to Bath. It seemed so nonsensical to keep one here when I knew there would be little opportunity to use it."

"Nor does Melanie have one," he replied. "Don't concern yourself. I'll engage to procure mounts for you."

A delighted Melanie assured Charles that he was the best of uncles, and plans were soon made for the expedition to take place on Monday.

Walking home a short time later, Elizabeth found that she was anticipating the coming event with an inordinate amount of eagerness. Of course, she was simply looking forward to the pleasure of riding once more, she told herself. It had nothing to do with the way Charles had held her hand for a moment longer than necessary, or with the way he had looked into her eyes as they said goodbye.

CHAPTER FIVE

LATER THAT NIGHT while preparing for bed, Elizabeth thought, not for the first time, how well she liked Charles Carlyle. He was certainly the most unusual man she had ever met. But try as she might, she could not fathom the reason for his behaviour towards her. The sudden thought that he might be trying to fix his interest with her made her gasp with alarm. If that were so, she must put a stop to it immediately!

In the next moment, however, she was able to dismiss the idea. After all, he was a confirmed bachelor as well as an unregenerate rake, and she was quite sure that he meant only to get up a flirtation with her, since he must find Bath a flat-out bore. At the same time, she felt that a harmless flirtation would do much to relieve her own growing sense of dissatisfaction and boredom. That he must soon enough depart for more intriguing climes she could not doubt, though why the thought of that inevitable event should have such a lowering effect on her spirits was a mystery. She did not stop to consider why he should have stayed even this long. Whatever the reason, his presence had brightened her rather dull existence, and she could not remember when she had felt so alive.

In the event, she did not see Charles for two days, until the Monday morning when they rode out with Melanie and her friends. The hacks he brought for them were first-rate animals, her own a lovely grey mare with excellent points, and Melanie's equally as fine. When he had helped her to mount, and they had all started off, Elizabeth and Charles fell a little behind the others.

She said, smiling up at him, "These are not hired hacks. They're prime 'uns, as Papa would have said. Wherever did you find them?"

"I have them on loan from a friend who lives not far from here."

"Oh, is that where you have been? I thought..."

No sooner had the words passed her lips than she wished to retrieve them, for his eyes crinkled with laughter as he said, "How very flattering. I believe you missed me."

"Certainly not!" she denied. "I would not have realized that you were gone had your sister not mentioned the fact."

"Ah! That's tipped me a settler! But where did you think I had been?"

"Well, Lady Claibourne was with us at the time, and I believe she said something about one of your chères amies."

"You put me to the blush, ma'am. What do you know about chères amies?"

In truth, she knew very little about this subject, her father not having considered it a necessary part of her masculine education, and she knew very well that she was the one blushing, but felt goaded into replying, "You may think me a green girl, but I promise you I am *not* just come from the schoolroom! I know quite well that a chère amie is a man's—is a woman of a certain class who—oh! I should not be saying these things! But how unhandsome of you to provoke me so!"

She frowned at him, but at the sight of his comically remorseful expression, she was unable to suppress a choke of laughter.

He grinned back at her, saying, "You are adorable!"

"No! I should not—"

"No, no!" he interrupted. "I beg you'll not turn missish on me. I detest insipid females and bland conversation. I wish you will leave your tongue unguarded when you are with me, for I find our talks vastly refreshing."

Her brow wrinkled in thought, and after a moment she answered, "Well, do you know, it is so very comfortable to have a friend with whom one may share one's thoughts and laughter without always having to worry about propriety. Papa was just such a friend to me, but in general I think such friends must be quite rare.''

There was an oddly arrested expression in his eyes as he responded, "Yes. Quite rare, indeed!''

They rode on for a few minutes without speaking, but at last she glanced sideways at him, and a flush crept into her cheeks again as she asked, "Are you really a shocking rake?''

"Alas, I fear I am," he said with mock sorrow. "A ramshackle fellow, sunk below reproach.''

"But what have you done to earn such a reputation?''

He looked rather startled. "You mean to take me at my word, don't you?''

She was still blushing faintly, but having screwed up her courage, she had no intention of backing down. "Yes, I do," she told him. "Well, you gave me leave to speak freely. But do you mean to answer my question?''

"I think not!''

Her eyes flew to his face, and found his expression a little grim. She said quickly, "Oh! I don't mean that I wish to hear all about your... your orgies, or your chères amies. But have you been *very* bad?''

He gave one of his shouts of laughter. "Minx! There have been no orgies, I promise you. Other than that, I shall tell you only that I don't make a habit of seducing ladies of quality, or of ravishing innocent maidens.'' Under his breath, too low for her to hear, he added, "At least, not intentionally."

Charles's thoughts went back to the one deeply regretted episode in his life when he had, indeed, seduced and ravished an innocent maiden.

He had had no intention, six years ago, of attending his sister's house party. He was far too familiar with her matchmaking propensities to allow himself to be trapped, for a sennight, with whatever simpering chit she proposed to throw in his way this time. To have done so he must have been a complete gudgeon. But then he had learned that Lady Sabina was a member of the party, and he had posted down from Town on the last night.

Lady Sabina was a promising little beauty with whom he had been carrying on his latest flirtation. Having broken off with the last in a long series of lovers, she had made it plain that she would not object to their own affair becoming more intimate.

He had arrived late, just as everyone was preparing to go to their beds, but he had managed to steal a few moments alone with Sabina. They had made an assignation, agreeing to meet in the summer house as soon as her husband should fall asleep. He had waited for nearly an hour before she finally came— at least, he had thought it was she.

When he realized his mistake, the unpardonable offense he'd committed—though what the devil an innocent girl was doing there in the middle of the night, he still didn't know!—well, he had meant to make things right with her in some way. But the silly chit had run off before he could learn who she was. He had strongly suspected her to be one of his sister's housemaids, and when, on the following morning, he saw that none of his fellow guests could possibly have been his unknown *fille de joie*, he decided he had been right. However, after a couple of awkward and rather embarrassing interviews with the only two maids who might have been she, he was as much in the dark as before. He had never been able to discover the identity of his mysterious little love. Lord! She had been something special, though!

While he had been preoccupied with these thoughts, Elizabeth had been considering what he had said and now, her brow furrowed, she asked, "Are you not accepted into the first circles? Is that why you've never wed?"

It was a moment before he could bring his thoughts back into the present, then he grinned and said, "Oh, it's not so bad as that. I assure you, I'm quite respectable enough, or at least have enough wealth, to be accepted into the first circles of Society. However, since I find the social code governing males and females tiresome in the extreme, and haven't the smallest desire to become a tenant for life, I try to avoid all the fashionable squeezes as much as possible."

She didn't understand why his lack of interest in marriage should discompose her, but so it did, and her smile was rather brittle as she said, "Well, that is fortunate, to be sure! Since I am not in want of a husband, and you are not hanging out for a wife, there is nothing to throw a rub in the way of a comfortable friendship between us."

"Indeed!" was all he replied, but a slight frown creased his brow.

They spoke only the merest commonplaces after that, until they arrived at their destination. The monument raised in honour of Sir Basil Grenville, and the nearby remains of a Saxon fortification were viewed with somewhat more enthusiasm by the younger members of the party than by Elizabeth and Charles. There was nothing more to be seen, and it was not long before they started on the return journey.

Elizabeth and Charles once again rode behind the others, and he was soon amusing her, and making her laugh with a story that was told of Lady Holland. They went on to discuss the Prince Regent's latest starts and their literary favourites, then lapsed into a companionable silence until Charles suddenly asked, "How is your estimable suitor?"

She glanced at him. "Lord Braxton?"

He studied her face, a slight smile upon his lips, but an odd, unreadable expression in his eyes. "Have you other suitors? I must warn you, my sweet, that we rakes are noted for our jealous and possessive natures.''

Disconcerted, she ignored his last statement. "No, of course I have no other suitors. Only Lord Braxton.''

"Have you not yet sent him to rout?''

"Would that I could! I am sure that I ought to like him, for he has so many admirable virtues, but I own that I cannot. Poor man!''

"Don't waste your sympathy on him,'' he advised her. "The man is a crushing bore and was born to be abused.''

"What an infamous thing to say!''

"Not at all. I'm convinced Lord Braxton and I have a mutual regard for each other. I'm sure he would like nothing better than to throw me in the close, if he were able to.''

"I collect that is a boxing term, and I'm woefully ignorant on that subject, I'm sorry to say.''

"No, no! Never apologize to a gentleman for being ignorant!''

"Never apologize for being ignorant?'' she asked, astonished. "Whatever do you mean?''

"Never to a gentleman, I said. There is no surer way for a female to fix a man's interest than by showing ignorance, and the more imbecilic the better in most cases. How else can a man puff off his better-informed mind and superior intelligence?''

"Oh! You are being absurd again!" She laughed. "And if you mean to instruct me in the art of boxing, I pray you will not! I haven't the least desire to learn it."

"My dear girl, with such an attitude you shall make me think you don't wish to attach me. I take leave to tell you that in all my dealings with you, you have shown a sad want of witlessness, and I suspect that has been your trouble all along."

She gave an indignant gasp, then struggled to keep from laughing, with little success.

"Abominable creature!" she accused.

"Adorable baggage!" he retaliated.

They went on in this way, talking easily with each other until they had nearly reached Bath, and Charles asked abruptly, "Who is this young smart who is being so attentive to my niece?"

Elizabeth glanced ahead to where an elegant young gentleman rode close beside Melanie and was in animated conversation with her. With a puzzled frown she turned her gaze back to Charles. "He is Adrian Kirby."

"I know that, my lovely goose. I should perhaps have asked, what do you know of him? Are you acquainted with him?"

"No, not well. I believe he is visiting his great-aunt, who is one of our Bath Quizzes. He has become quite friendly with the Gilberts, and appears to be a very amiable, well-mannered young man. Why do you ask? Do you fear that he isn't a fit beau for her?"

"No. I was simply curious." He grinned as he added, "One cannot be too careful when one is a chaperon."

"Oh, dear! I fear I have been sadly remiss in my duties. I never noticed that he was trying to make himself so agreeable to her."

"Don't fret, my sweet. You may be a deplorable chaperon, but you are an excellent companion," he teased.

By this time they were in Bath, and after leaving the others at Laura Place, Charles rode with Elizabeth to Upper Camden Place. When they arrived, he dismounted, and tethered the horses before coming to her side to help her. But instead of handing her down in the way she expected, he placed both hands on her slim waist and lifted her down, then stood for a moment looking into her eyes, his hands still on her waist.

He released her at last and said quietly, "It has been a delightful day."

"Oh, yes," she answered breathlessly, for she suddenly felt very confused and very shy.

CHAPTER SIX

AFTER THEIR PARTING that afternoon, both Elizabeth and Charles experienced some misgivings at the intensity of their feelings in that moment. However, each managed, after a period of introspection, to subdue what fears they had that there might be some danger in continuing the acquaintance. Both contrived to convince themselves that they were capable of keeping their association on the level of a friendly flirtation.

And so, when Charles called the next day, inviting Elizabeth to ride out with him, she agreed without a qualm, and over the next two weeks, they spent increasingly more time together, taking long rides over the countryside, meeting in the Pump Room and in Sydney Gardens, or walking out to Beechen Cliff. They attended the balls in the assembly rooms, the concerts on Wednesday evenings and dined together often with their families.

Elizabeth, having decided simply to enjoy this interlude in her quiet life, stepped forward to meet each new day joyously and heedlessly, blind to the knowing looks of all the Bath Quizzes, and deaf to their tongue-waggings. Nor did she take notice of the frequent concern that began to show in her aunt's eyes.

A strong sense of uneasiness and fear was developing in Emily's breast. At first, thrown into transports of joy by the apparent affinity between her niece and Charles, she had congratulated Margaret on whatever contrivance she had used to prolong Charles's presence in Bath. And when her friend had denied any hand in this, Emily became quite deliriously hopeful of the desired outcome of the affair, surmising that Elizabeth was the attraction which held him. So wildly optimistic was she that she had allowed them hours alone together without protest or consideration for propriety. She had even gone so far as to encourage this very improper conduct.

But Emily could not fail for long to see the sidelong glances, or hear the whispered innuendoes of Bath Society. Neither could she forget Charles's unfortunate reputation, nor the fact that he had never yet shown any predilection for serious or lasting romantic connections.

At last, she could contain her dire apprehensions no longer and revealed them to her friend.

"But, Margaret," she wailed, "it has been more than two weeks, and while they are forever in each other's pockets, and he is excessively attentive, I cannot but feel that his manner is more flirtatious than overwise."

"Nonsense, Emily!" her friend replied. "It is as plain as a pikestaff that they are head over heels in love. They are simply too foolish or too obstinate to admit to it."

"Do you think so, indeed?" asked Emily hopefully.

"Of course! Stop being such a ninnyhammer, Emily!"

However, Emily could not stop being what she was and very soon fell prey, once more, to the most miserable doubts.

"Still, if he should be but amusing himself with a mere flirtation, it would be too unbearably dreadful! Oh, I don't know what I should do!"

"I daresay what they need is a small push and I expect we must give it," Lady Margaret mused.

"It's all very well for you to say that, but I cannot for the life of me see what we may do!"

The veriest touch of peevishness had crept into Emily's voice.

"Well, my dear, I had not meant to tell you quite yet, but as it happens, I do have a scheme that just may answer," said the redoubtable Lady Langley.

When she failed to continue, but sat instead in frowning contemplation, Emily urged impatiently, "Well? What is it? Don't just sit there! Pray, tell me!"

Her affectionate friend had no intention of disclosing her plan to Emily too soon. The dear, silly feather-brain would more than likely let the cat out of the bag by telling Elizabeth, so she said, "No, don't ask me, for I shan't tell you yet. I must still work out a few minor details, but when I have done, I shall not hesitate to tell you the whole. Trust me, my dear."

And with that Emily was obliged to be satisfied.

It was but three days later, while Elizabeth was out walking with Charles, that Wiggons again led Lady Langley to the morning room in Upper Camden Place. She waited only until the butler had left them before saying, "Emily, we have not a moment to lose! We must put my scheme to the test today. I'll not deny that I had hoped for more time to think it through. However, a remark Charles made last night makes me fear that he means to leave Bath any day now."

"Oh, I knew it! I knew it!" cried Emily, falling back into her chair dramatically, hands pressed to her heart.

"Do spare me your starts, Emily! Good heavens! We haven't time for your vapours and spasms now! Come down to the drawing room and I'll explain my plan to you."

Lady Langley assisted the bewildered, wilting Emily from her chair and led her down to the drawing room, adjusting her trailing shawl for her as they went, and soon had her installed on the sofa, vinaigrette in hand.

Speaking carefully, as though to a child, she said, "Now then, my dear, I must just have a word with Wiggons and then I'll explain everything. In the meantime, simply continue as you are and you shall play your part to perfection." Then she hurried from the room.

A half hour later, at eleven o'clock, Elizabeth and Charles were standing at the door, saying goodbye, when it was opened to reveal Wiggons who, with his usual aplomb, intoned, "Miss Elizabeth, if you please, Lady Langley is waiting in the drawing room and requests that both you and the gentleman attend her there as soon as may be."

He held the door wide for them, and the pair, exchanging questioning looks, crossed the entry hall and threw open the door to the drawing room.

The spectacle which awaited them was wholly astonishing. Emily lay prostrate upon the sofa, one arm flung across her eyes, vinaigrette clutched in the other hand, moaning softly. Lady Langley was lying back in a deep wing-chair, one foot elevated upon a small stool, a mixture of pain and distress contorting her features.

Lady Langley opened her eyes and said faintly, "Oh, Charles! Thank God you are come!"

"Good God!" he exclaimed. "What has happened?"

Elizabeth had rushed to her aunt's side in apprehensive solicitude, but Emily only moaned more piteously in answer to her alarmed questions.

Lady Langley uttered a small, anguished cry as she shifted the position of her foot, but gazed bravely up at her brother, saying in the same dying voice, "No, no, my dear, do not fear for me. It's nothing. Merely a severe sprain which I incurred upon the doorstep in my haste to get here. And though the pain is quite excruciating, I daresay I shall bear up."

"But what is this? How came you to be in such haste to get here?"

"Oh, Charles! What shall I do? My poor Melanie! How could she be so lost to all sense of propriety? Oh, what am I to do?"

She was wringing her hands anxiously, and Emily's moans increased in volume as Charles, running his hand through his hair, demanded, "What the devil are you talking about? And how am I to tell you what should be done until I can make sense of what you are saying? Come now! Tell me the story with no more roundaboutation."

"Oh, Charles," his sister cried tragically, "Melanie has eloped with Adrian Kirby! I was never so deceived or so ill-used!"

"Damnation! Are you sure?"

"Well, of course I am sure! Why should I tell you such a tale if it were not true?"

Emily moaned loudly.

"How the devil do you know?" asked Charles reasonably, though with some impatience.

From her reticule she pulled a sheet of paper which was covered with nearly illegible handwriting and spotted liberally with what appeared to be tear stains. Charles gave it only a cursory glance, as his sister said, "You may well stare! I did myself when I saw this note!"

"What in God's name can have possessed the tiresome chit to do anything so idiotically bird-witted?" Charles demanded.

"Oh, there isn't time for that!" Lady Margaret wailed. "She shall be ruined if she isn't stopped! Oh, Charles, you must go after her!"

"Yes, of course," he replied, scowling, and ran his fingers through his hair once more. "We must assume them to be making for Gretna Green. Have you a map, Elizabeth?"

"I shall fetch it, Charles," Elizabeth said, hurrying from the room.

Noting this intimate use of their given names, Lady Margaret just barely stifled a crow of satisfaction, and admirably preserved her agonized countenance.

When Elizabeth returned, she and Charles pored over the map.

"They will be taking the Bristol turnpike. It's the only decent one if one wishes to travel quickly," she told him.

Glancing up at his sister, he asked tersely, "How long have they been gone?"

"It cannot have been above an hour. You should catch them easily if you hurry."

"Yes," he said, and folding the map, he started for the door.

"Stay!" shouted Lady Langley, arresting him on the spot.

"What the devil?" he exclaimed irritably.

"Oh, Charles, I am persuaded that my poor girl would wish to have a female to lend her support when you catch up with them. But what shall we do? Neither Emily nor I are in any case to go with you. And her abigail would be no better than useless. She is so very shatter-brained!"

"I shall be happy to go with him, ma'am," said Elizabeth. "We should overtake them easily in time to be back before nightfall."

"Oh, my dear, would you? I cannot thank you enough!"

"Yes, of course. I should like to help."

Elizabeth looked to Charles for his approval of this plan, but he was studying his sister speculatively.

After a moment a faint smile curled his lips and he said, "Of course. The perfect solution."

Turning to Elizabeth, he told her, "I believe we shall travel much faster in my curricle than in a closed carriage. I shall fetch it while you are changing into warmer clothing. It will be a cold drive."

Elizabeth ran to do his bidding, and Charles faced his sister once again. "Take heart, dear sister," he said with a grin. "Somehow I feel sure all will go as you wish!"

He saluted her once and was gone.

Elizabeth was waiting in her warmest gown and pelisse, carrying a fur muff to warm her hands, when he returned in a half hour. After handing her up and placing a lap-robe over her knees, he climbed up beside her and, flicking the reins, started off.

They were soon racing out of the town.

Elizabeth, caught up in the dire urgency of their errand, failed to see Lord Braxton standing on the street corner near her home. He was staring after them, a look of profound disapproval on his face.

CHAPTER SEVEN

ELIZABETH AT FIRST forebore saying anything, not wishing to divert Charles's attention from his driving, since she thought that very likely his concern for his niece would already have distracted him quite enough. No more than two miles had sped by, however, until she realized that Charles, whom she knew to be an excellent whip, was driving to an inch, his expert handling of the reins in no way affected by anxiety—for Melanie or anything else. In fact, one might almost have supposed that he was quite enjoying himself, for an almost imperceptible smile curved his mouth and the tiny creases at the corner of his one visible eye seemed more pronounced.

At that moment, he turned his head to glance down at her, and she thought she must have been mistaken in that first impression.

His expression now held nothing but the kindest solicitude as he asked, "Are you quite warm enough?"

She smiled up at him. "Oh, yes. How kind it was of you to have provided a hot brick for my feet. Thank you!"

"Not at all. However, we have a distance to go and the brick will not remain hot forever. If you should begin to feel the cold, I trust you will tell me."

"Well, I shall, but I confess I am at a loss to know what you might do about it."

"I shall give you my coat, of course."

She admired the dashing driving coat he wore, with its several capes, as she said, "How unchivalrous of me that would be! So I am to take your coat and leave you to freeze, am I?"

"Oh, I won't freeze, I assure you! I'm seldom bothered by the cold. However, should I find myself in that unhappy predicament, we may easily find the remedy."

"Yes, by returning your coat to you instantly!"

"No, no! I would not be so shabby as to offer you the protection of my coat, only to take it back again. What a poor opinion you must have of me! No, I would simply require you to nestle close to me. That should do the trick."

The mischievous gleam in his eyes made her laugh, and she retorted, "Very likely! But I wish you would be serious!" Then, the tone of her voice obeying her own suggestion, she continued, "Do you know, I find this elopement puzzling in the extreme, now I've had time to think on it. Mr. Kirby has certainly been most attentive to Melanie, but no more so than several other young men. However, I had not thought that she liked him above any of the others. Besides which, she is forever talking about her London come-out, so why should she suddenly wish to elope? It is the oddest thing."

"Yes, isn't it?"

She looked at him, frowning. "And here is another puzzle, for you don't appear to be in the least disturbed by all this!"

"No? Well, perhaps not. After all—who knows?—we may be wronging the girl. At all events, let us withhold judgement until we know the whole."

"Do you say that she may have some excuse for such outrageous behaviour?"

"Not at all."

"Then I am at a loss as to what you may mean!"

"I would rather not say at present. My thoughts on the matter may be completely mistaken."

She could get no more from him and they drove on in silence, only making desultory remarks now and then until they reached Bristol, where Charles made discreet enquiries.

As he climbed back into the curricle and they started off once more, he said, "No one remembers seeing them. But then they may have stopped here."

This failure did not worry Elizabeth unduly, but when they received no news of the runaway couple at either the Church End turnpike, or any other stop along the way, she began to feel a distinct uneasiness. They had passed only a few private coaches along the road, and in none of these had they perceived the youthful elopers. To make matters worse, the sky was becoming more overcast with each mile that they travelled.

Charles allayed some of her fears when he said, "The fact that no one remembers seeing them means nothing. It is difficult to make adequate enquiries when I am unable even to describe their carriage."

This made sense and she still believed that this was the only reasonable road for the young couple to have taken, but what if they had not? The Bristol turnpike was in much better condition for fast travel than the alternative road, but it was not, after all, the shortest route.

Not all of Charles's reassurances could banish her dread entirely, however, especially when a light snow began to fall a few miles out of Gloucester. It was a little past three o'clock then, and Charles pulled into the yard of a small inn called, appropriately, The Bird in Hand. They had changed horses only once along the way, and these could go no further. An ostler hastened out immediately to take charge of the pair, and Charles sprang down and spoke to him quietly for a few moments before coming back to Elizabeth. "Come," he said, "we'll go in and thaw out."

As he reached to hand her down, she stared at him in amazement. By now, it was quite clear to her that their mission was hopeless. It was equally clear from the lowering sky that darkness would fall much sooner than normal. Concern for the change in the weather, added to her fears for Melanie, were setting her on edge, and Charles's nonchalance caused her to speak more sharply than she intended. "But what are you about? It is perfectly obvious that we must turn back if we are to reach Bath before nightfall. And I am persuaded that we must do so at once!"

"My dear, we are going nowhere just now, except inside this inn, where we will warm ourselves and have some refreshments. Then we will discuss what must be done."

Since she was so frightfully cold by now that it required the most exacting effort to prevent her teeth chattering, she gave in with tolerable good grace.

The landlord greeted them cheerfully and obsequiously, for he knew quality when he saw it, and was pleased to offer his best private parlour to the gentleman and his sister when Charles requested it. If he thought it odd behaviour for a gentleman to carry his sister on a journey, in this weather, in an open carriage, and with little or no baggage—well, there was no accounting for what the quality might do. He bowed them into a comfortable-appearing room and while he bustled about, starting a fire to warm them, Charles helped Elizabeth remove her pelisse and bonnet and seated her in one of the wingchairs beside the fireplace. He then excused himself and followed the landlord from the room.

He returned just as the waiter, carrying a tray which contained a bottle of wine, a pot of tea and some cold meats, arrived. When they were seated at the table, Elizabeth said, "I must own that some tea will be very welcome, but I don't care to eat anything."

"Nonsense! You haven't eaten since this morning. It will do us no good if you faint from hunger later on. Come, you'll feel more the thing after a few bites."

She was annoyed at being obliged to admit, again, that he was right, but as she could see the wisdom of his words, she once more acquiesced and placed some food on her plate. Before she had taken her second bite, she found that she had been far hungrier than she had thought, and they both set about the business of eating in silence.

When she had finished, she looked up to see that Charles had turned his chair sideways and was sitting at his ease, one arm resting on the table, his long, shapely legs stretched out before him, his booted feet crossed at the ankles. He was watching her with a peculiar expression, impossible to read, and with a slight smile upon his lips.

She returned his smile and said, "Well, you were right, of course. I feel much better now and am ready to leave whenever you are. Naturally, we shall not get back before nightfall, but I am persuaded that we need not regard that."

His eyes remained fixed on her face as he picked up his wineglass and sipped from it before answering her. "My dear," he said apologetically, "I hardly know how to tell you this, but I have engaged rooms for us here, for the night."

She stared at him, too shocked to be capable of speech.

He continued softly, "If you will but think, you will realize that I could do nothing else. Were the weather more agreeable, we *might* make it back with no insurmountable difficulty. However, with this snow it would be the height of folly to attempt it."

"Oh, but a few snowflakes—what can they signify? They cannot continue for long!"

He smiled ruefully. "If you will but look out of that window behind you, you shall see that you are mistaken."

She turned her head towards the window, then jumped up and ran to it. What had been, on their arrival, a few flurries, was now a full-fledged blizzard, with the wind driving a heavy curtain of snow before it. The ground was covered, and she realized that she had been hearing the whistling of the wind for some time without being aware of it.

"Oh! Of course we cannot leave," she cried. Then, after a few moments she turned and murmured, "How foolish of me. I can't seem to think clearly."

He had followed her to the window, and now placed his hands on her shoulders. For just an instant she thought he meant to take her in his arms, and felt an almost overwhelming desire to take the one small step that would permit her to melt against him and lay her head on his chest. Instead, after a small hesitation, he took her hand, led her to her chair by the fireplace and gently urged her into it before moving to the other.

"My poor girl," he said tenderly, "you have endured a great deal today, have you not?"

She sat upright in her chair, hands folded in her lap, and said, "It's the most absurd thing. I'm perfectly sure I ought to be concerned about any number of things, but all I seem able to think is that I have no change of clothes or even any tooth powder."

He grinned rather uneasily, for all the world as though he were a small boy guilty of mischief, as he said, "Well, do you know, it is one of my excessively strange habits that I like to be prepared for all eventualities. Before leaving the house, I had Melanie's abigail throw a few of her things into a portmanteau. Of course, the gown may be a trifle short, and there is no tooth powder."

She wrinkled her brow. "How very odd of you. How—"

He interrupted hastily, "And perhaps I can relieve at least one other of your concerns by telling you that I have no intention of taking advantage of our situation to ravish you!''

"Oh, no! I know you would not! What a shabby trick that would be to play on a friend!"

He threw his head back and laughed. "You are delightful! And if I had had the dastardly intention of playing you false, in spite of my promise, that sentiment would put paid to it."

She answered his grin, sinking back into her chair, and they sat quietly for a time, watching the flames of the fire.

At last Charles stood and went to the table. "Would you care for a glass of wine, my dear? Or would you prefer that I call for some ratafia?"

"The wine, please." She smiled.

He poured two glasses and carried them back to the fire, handed her one and seated himself again.

She took a sip before suddenly exclaiming. "Oh! We have not given one thought to poor Melanie! I wonder where she may be."

His mouth twisted sardonically. "If my theory is correct, poor Melanie is just where she ought to be—in Bath with her mother!"

She looked astonished. "I beg your pardon, but I seem to be more than usually dull-witted today. I don't understand you!"

He hesitated before asking what seemed an irrelevant question. "My sweet, is your aunt pleased with your apparent preference for the single state?"

"Oh, no!" she laughed. "She is forever scolding me and lamenting over it."

"Well, my own dear sister is not only of the same mind where I am concerned, but is also an inveterate matchmaker, and a schemer of the first water, to boot—with few scruples to her credit!"

"Good God! You cannot mean what I think you do! That Lady Langley and Aunt Emily planned this whole contretemps? No! I cannot credit it! It would be too insane—too monstrous of them!" Then she added triumphantly, "And besides, they couldn't possibly have known that it would come on to snow and trap us here."

"I will own that I'm still puzzled by that aspect of it," he said. "Well, perhaps you have the right of it. And if that is so, then Melanie is indeed on her way to Gretna Green and an elopement, and there is nothing we can do to prevent it." He paused for a moment, frowning. "In which case, I only hope that it is, in fact, marriage that Mr. Kirby has in mind."

Elizabeth stared at him. "Oh, but surely—"

"There is nothing sure about it," he interrupted. "What do we know of this Adrian Kirby? A marriage over the anvil would be disastrous enough, but if he should merely be bent on seduction, Melanie will most certainly be ruined. No decent man would be willing to offer her marriage after such an event."

Gazing into his wineglass, Charles failed to see how Elizabeth's face paled. This was much too close to her own situation, and though his assessment of the outcome agreed with her own, she could not prevent herself from asking, "But if the man loved her...?"

"My dear," he said quietly, "no man wishes to take another man's leavings."

She drew a sharp breath and colour rushed back into her cheeks. She had always accepted the truth of what he'd said, but even so, such a typically male opinion struck her as being blatantly unfair, and she cried, "That is ridiculous! It is my understanding that men do so nearly every time they take a mistress!"

"That is a different matter entirely. I was speaking of marriage," he replied rather sternly. Then his face relaxed into a smile as he continued, "But there is no need for us to discompose ourselves over such an unlikely occurrence. As I said before, I strongly suspect that Melanie is even now with her mother."

Fearing that her own past experience had prompted her to respond overemphatically, Elizabeth made a deliberate attempt to calm herself and turn her thoughts to their previous conversation. Several moments passed before she was successful, but then her eyes opened wide with dawning comprehension.

"Charles! If you really thought my aunt and your sister capable of such deviousness, you are as bad as you would have me believe them to be. Worse! For, believing it, you still went along with it! Oh!—and you even brought a change of clothes! How could you?''

"No, no! Don't be so quick to rip up at me! I only *suspected* it to be an underhanded plot. That being so, it was incumbent upon me to proceed with it, in case Melanie should actually be eloping. As for the change of clothes, who can say what may happen along the road? We might have lost a wheel, or one of the horses might have gone lame. Oh, any number of things might have gone awry. And I did mention, did I not, that I like to be prepared.''

She cast a suspicious look at him, but offered no further arguments, and they continued sipping their wine and gazing into the fire. She had lost track of time when Charles looked at his watch.

"I think, my dear, that we should repair to our bedchambers to refresh ourselves. I thought, too, that perhaps it would be wise to have an early dinner and retire early to bed. It has been a long and exhausting day.''

She agreed and started towards the door, but just as she reached it he touched her arm to detain her.

"One moment, please. You will remember, I hope, that I have told the landlord that you are my sister?''

"That was clever of you. Yes, I'll remember.''

They climbed the stairs together, going to their separate bedchambers, and after splashing cold water on her face, Elizabeth felt a great deal refreshed. That done, she opened her reticule to find her comb and froze, staring bemusedly, for there in full view was her tooth powder. Only Aunt Emily could have put it there, and the knowledge came instantly that Charles's theory had, indeed, been correct.

Those damnably wretched women! How could they have played such a despicable trick? It was certain that they had hoped to force her and Charles into marriage, and for a moment Elizabeth considered what it might be like to spend a lifetime with him. She was a little shocked to realize that the notion was far from unpleasant and even more shocked to realize the reason for that. How long had she been in love with him?

CHAPTER EIGHT

FEELING SUDDENLY as though her legs would no longer hold her up, Elizabeth sat down abruptly on the edge of the bed.

For several moments, her mind was blank, her brain seemingly paralyzed by the stunning effect of her momentous discovery, and when it began to function again, one refrain ran through it repeatedly. *She loved him.* She loved Charles, loved him with all her heart and soul, and would give all she possessed if only she could be his wife. For a short while she was filled with a sense of wonder and joy.

But what was she thinking of? She could not marry Charles without first telling him of her own less-than-virtuous state, and how could she tell him when he had proven to be such a high stickler—a veritable prig, according to his sister—when it came to marriage and ladies of quality. Besides, she did not wish to give up her prized freedom and independence, did she? No! Of course not, she told herself firmly. But then, why was she feeling this ridiculous urge to weep?

In order to hold such traitorous feelings at bay, she reminded herself that Charles had no desire to marry, and furthermore, he had, only a short time earlier, implicitly recalled to her the fact that no man would wish to take her to wife. She felt a reviving surge of anger at that injustice, but it was soon followed by another wave of sadness. If only Charles . . .

She shook her head in self-disgust. It was madness for her to be entertaining these thoughts. She would be much better occupied in attempting to find a way out of this muddle. Thank heaven, Charles had had the great good sense to say that she was his sister. They would come about somehow.

Suddenly aware of the passage of time, she quickly ran the comb through her curls, arranging them in a simple style, and not knowing whether to feel relieved or regretful, she descended to the parlour where Charles awaited her.

The dinner presently served them proved to be passably good, but was consumed with less appreciation than it might conceivably have received had their minds not been otherwise engaged.

It was not until they were once again ensconced before the fire that Charles, lazily regarding the flames through his brandy glass, said casually, "I wonder, my dear, if you fully realize all the implications of our predicament."

"By all means! I am not stupid! I'm well aware that it will require the greatest care if we are to avoid

a scandal. At the least, there may be some specula-
tion, I suppose, but I shan't regard that." She smiled
brightly to show him how little she regarded it.

"My foolish, naive girl. There is only one thing to
be done. You must marry me."

For several moments, Elizabeth simply looked at
Charles, surprised that he sounded so composed, so
undisturbed. Then, as she realized that he was waiting for her answer, she insisted, "Oh, no! What
nonsense! That isn't at all necessary. I shall say that
I have been visiting friends overnight."

He frowned. "Now *that* is nonsense! I fear it will
be an impossibility to keep the truth hidden. Too
many people are aware of it: your aunt, my sister,
Wiggons—and if he knows, very likely all the servants do. Furthermore, there is no saying who may
have seen us drive out of town together." He reached
for her hand, saying more gently, "Surely you must
see that there is no other way. You *must* marry me."

"No! I am persuaded that it is not necessary!" she
cried.

He had remained fairly calm up to this point, but
impatience was now evident in the way he ran his
hand through his hair and sounded clearly in his
voice as he said, "If you do not regard the damage
to your own reputation, then you might consider *my*
feelings in the matter. For I'll tell you, in no uncer-
tain terms, my girl, that I don't intend to have it said

of me that I compromised you and did not marry you!"

Her chin lifted stubbornly. "I suppose I should feel honoured that you are willing to make such a great sacrifice on my behalf, but I cannot allow it. I shall no doubt survive any damage to my reputation, and I should think that your reputation as a rake could only be enhanced."

"You are being foolish beyond belief!" he returned irritably. "I had no idea that you would find the thought of marriage to me so repugnant!"

"Oh, no! I do not!" she cried, unwilling to allow him to believe that it was him she rejected. "It is the thought of marriage itself that I find repugnant."

He stared at her in disbelief. "I find such a statement from any female astounding! Unless— No, never mind."

It had occurred to him that she was speaking of the physical intimacy implied by marriage and that it was this which she found distasteful. Good God! He would never have thought it of her. She had so much liveliness and warmth in her character that it was difficult to credit that she might be cold in that respect.

His frowning gaze was beginning to make Elizabeth uncomfortable, and finally she said, "Well, I am glad that you have decided to be sensible about this. I shall think of another way."

"Don't be idiotic!" was his terse rejoinder. "I have not changed my mind, and if your chin gets any higher, you are going to put a permanent crick in your neck!"

"Oh!" she breathed, glaring at him. "Well, neither have I changed my mind!"

They sat there exchanging glares until, unexpectedly, Charles began to laugh. Though at first she was incensed that he could find their argument amusing, it was not long until a smile began to tug at her own mouth.

At last, Charles, wiping tears of mirth from his eyes, said, "I believe we are having our first fight, my love," and as she opened her mouth to answer, he stopped her with "No, no! Let us cry quit for tonight. I've no wish to come to cuffs with you. We are both tired and will do better to postpone this discussion until tomorrow."

Elizabeth had to agree with him. "Very well. Until tomorrow, then. And if you do not mind, I think that I shall retire now."

"Certainly, my dear," he answered, and walked her to the door, where he placed both hands on her shoulders and dropped a light kiss on her forehead.

She murmured a hasty "Good night" and hurried from the room before he could see the devastating effect that innocent kiss had had upon her. Charles stood there for a moment, a thoughtful expression on his face before going up to his own chamber.

Soon after meeting Elizabeth, he had admitted to himself that the very first sight of her had tipped him a leveller, and that had never happened to him before. But he had convinced himself that he could enjoy a brief flirtation with her, and then go on his way with neither of them the worse for it. It was not long before he knew that he was deceiving himself.

To become serious over any female, no matter how entrancing she might be, had never been part of his plan for the future, and when he began to suspect just how deeply he was coming to care for Elizabeth, his instinct had been to hare off to Brentwood, putting as much distance between them as possible. However, it was not his way to run from anything or anyone. And so he had stayed, and had become more besotted with her each day, which had forced him to re-examine his disinclination to become leg-shackled. Was it possible that his aversion had become nothing more than habit?

He knew that his chief motive for shunning marriage had always been the fact that he had never found a female who did not bore or disgust him within a very short time of meeting her. In his considerable experience, chaste females tended to fall into one of two categories. They were either insufferably insipid, brainless chits, or they were stiff-necked pattern cards of propriety. Even more intolerable were those less-than-chaste females who masqueraded as ladies of quality. At least the lightskirts of his acquaintance had the virtue of honesty—with regard to whom and what they were—to recommend them.

However, far from boring or disgusting him—and he could not imagine her ever doing so—Elizabeth attracted him in every way. In truth, she suited him very well. She was well-born and undoubtedly virtuous; a complete lady, in fact. She was also intelligent, witty and had a marvellous sense of humour. And if that weren't enough, she was an utter delight to look upon.

Having got so far in his deliberations, he then admitted that perhaps his sister was not so very wrong. Perhaps it *was* time that he married and set up his nursery. He was, after all, the last living male of his line. It might not be a bad thing to produce an heir to carry on the family name.

Yes, he thought, as he climbed into bed, for several days past he had been toying with the notion of offering for Elizabeth. His only problem had been in deciding how to overcome her peculiar resistance to the married state, and Margaret had provided the means of doing so. He did not expect too much opposition from Elizabeth, in spite of her behaviour this evening. And as for her fear of the physical aspects of marriage, it was doubtlessly no more than any innocent female might be expected to feel. It needed only patience and sensitivity on his part to allay it.

He smiled contentedly as his eyes drifted closed. *His son,* he mused, and the thought gave him unexpected pleasure. *His and Elizabeth's son . . .*

That thought gave him even more pleasure.

CHAPTER NINE

IT WAS LONG before Elizabeth was able to fall asleep that night, so many thoughts and questions were swirling through her brain.

How could she have allowed herself to fall in love with Charles and not have been aware of it? Now, of course, it was glaringly clear to her that there had been any number of clues which should have warned her. She supposed that deep down in her innermost self she *had* known, but to have admitted it to herself would have meant having to stop seeing him, and *that* she had been unwilling to do. And so she had deceived herself, never foreseeing where it might land her.

She ought to have seen through the machinations of those two conniving women—and had she had the wits of a two-year-old, she would have. Charles obviously had. And what, in the name of all that was holy, was he about? Since he had made no secret of his distaste for marriage, it was inconceivable that he should wish for it now. She unhesitatingly declined to believe that he could have fallen in love with her. No, it was as he had said: his concern for Melanie had prompted him to take part in this charade, and his notion of proper conduct now prompted him to offer for her.

She thought of his reaction when she had rejected his offer and wondered at it. She would have thought that he would leap at the opportunity to be let off the hook, but perhaps it was simply that the alternative she had suggested did not satisfy his sense of propriety. She still believed that to say she had spent the night with a friend would answer quite nicely, but if it did not suit him, she must come up with something better. But what?

After considerable reflection, she still had not found an answer and finally, exhausted, she gave up the attempt. Something was bound to occur to her tomorrow when she was more rested. Of course, if Charles persisted in his unnecessary notion of gallantry, she would be obliged to tell him the truth about herself. That truth, however, would only be used as a last resort. She did not think that she could bear it to have Charles consider her what he had called "another man's leavings."

On that unhappy thought, she finally fell into a restless sleep and did not awaken until ten o'clock the following morning when the landlady came into her room bearing hot water to wash with and coals for the fire.

A good-natured, amply endowed woman, neatly dressed and with a crisp, white cap tied under her chin, the innkeeper's wife kept up a running commentary as she busied herself about the room.

"Happen we have another lady and gentleman staying with us, or I would have sent you our Alice—she being our maid, you see. But I bethought myself that you, miss, and your gentleman brother, being quality, like, it was more fitting that I should be waiting upon you myself—and happy I am to be doing it! Not but what they don't be quality themselves, but there be quality and there be *quality*, I always say," said she, as she pulled back the curtains. "Lor' bless us, miss, just look at that! You'll not be going anywhere today. It's still snowing something fierce out there."

It needed only a glance to convince Elizabeth that this was nothing less than the truth, and she was sunk with dismay, but the landlady's cheerful monologue continued without pause.

"There's been nothing like it since I can't remember when. Happen it's been years since there's been such a snowfall, and all the roads closed with nothing able to get through. I shouldn't wonder if you was to be stuck here for a sennight. But there now, miss. I make no doubt you'll be wanting to make yourself all pretty-like, and best you do it while the water is nice and hot. You'll be wishful of having your breakfast, too, I make no doubt, which it'll be ready in a trice, and if you was wishful of anything else, miss, you have only to tell me."

She had whisked up Elizabeth's gown as she spoke and now bore it to the door with her. "I'll just be taking this downstairs to press, miss, and it'll be right as a trivet in no time at all, and back up to you before you know it."

When the door had closed behind her, Elizabeth continued to lie there for a few minutes. The protracted snowfall presented a definite problem. The longer they were kept here, the less likely it was that Charles would agree to any solution to their dilemma other than marriage. He must, however, and she must think of something that would make him see reason. But the only ideas that came to her were so idiotic that even she could not accept them.

Well, it made no sense for her to delay like this, she thought, and she forced herself out of bed and hurriedly performed her chilly ablutions. By the time she was ready for it, the landlady had sent her freshly pressed gown up to her, and she was soon satisfied that she made a presentable appearance.

When she entered the parlour, Charles was there before her, standing by the window, looking out. When she shut the door, he turned, smiling, and said, "Good morning," and with a gesture towards the window, added, "Have you had a chance to notice the weather? It looks as though we are likely to be tied here for some considerable time."

"Good morning," she answered, coming to stand beside him. "Yes, I saw it from my chamber as soon as I awoke."

The wind had died down, but the snow was still descending heavily, and for several minutes they stood watching it. She was afraid that he would re-open their discussion on matrimony and the evils of their situation, but he did not, and silence prevailed until their breakfast arrived.

While the landlady was in the room, conversation between them was impossible as she was no sooner through the door than she was embarked on one of her lengthy speeches. And when they were once more alone, and Charles merely remarked that he was famished, seated her and began filling their plates, she began to hope that he had no intention of reviving their disagreement.

She relaxed as the meal progressed and still he did not bring up the subject, engaging her instead in light-hearted banter, and discussing various means by which they might stave off boredom and make the time pass more quickly.

"We might try our hands at building a snow creature later on, if this lets up," he told her, grinning. "I used to be quite adept at it."

"Oh, Charles, yes! It sounds like great fun!"

He laughed softly at her enthusiasm, then said ruefully, "Yes, well, I should imagine we shall both be pining for something to do before many hours have passed.''

But it was not until the following afternoon that the snowfall lightened enough for them to venture out into it, and, surprisingly, time did not hang heavily over them for the remainder of that day. As always, they found a great deal to talk about, and had long, fascinating discussions on every subject imaginable, from the profound to the ridiculous.

The only worrisome thing for Elizabeth was the fact that not once did Charles raise the subject of their predicament. While she could not help but wonder at this, feeling that it was unnatural and only a temporary reprieve, still she was grateful. She continued to find herself at a standstill so far as a solution to their problem was concerned, and she had no wish to get into a skirmish with him over the matter.

They were again saved from boredom the next morning by the landlady, who had unearthed an old pack of playing cards and two books. The cards they agreed to save for a later time, and passed the morning hours reading, but by afternoon they had both had their fill of the small parlour and were more than ready to brave the snow and the cold.

Elizabeth had not had so much fun in years and threw herself into their venture with the abandon of the very young. They built their snowman and laughingly pelted one another with snowballs, behaving like children until the cold finally drove them back inside.

It was as they were playfully brushing snow from each other, just after entering the inn, that they first encountered their fellow guests, a Mr. and Mrs. Parker. The couple introduced themselves and Mrs. Parker remarked, "You are brother and sister? Oh, yes, I believe the innkeeper's wife did mention that fact." She looked from one to the other and Elizabeth stiffened slightly at the knowing look in her eyes as she continued, "How very odd. You do not at all resemble each other."

Charles smiled easily as he replied, "People frequently remark upon it, don't they, sister? But the fact is that we each take after different sides of the family."

"Really! How very interesting," said Mrs. Parker, and without pause, went on to say, "We were also told that you arrived in a curricle. Surely you could not have travelled far, in so open a vehicle, in this dreadful weather. Do you live nearby?"

"Not far," said Elizabeth shortly, disliking the woman and her vulgar inquisitiveness intensely.

"Oh...well! *We* were on our way to Bath when we were delayed by this wretched snow. Do you know Bath?"

"Slightly," said Charles. "And now, Mrs. Parker, I don't mean to be rude, but my sister and I must change out of these damp clothes before we catch our deaths.''

Elizabeth could feel the woman's avid gaze on their backs all the way up the stairs. Mr. Parker had said not a word during the entire exchange, and she could only wish that his wife had been as taciturn. She fully expected Charles to say something now, but he said nothing other than to recommend that she change into dry clothing as quickly as possible, before he went on to his own chamber.

Perversely, rather than feeling relieved, she felt quite irritable. She was on tenterhooks, as though waiting for a second shoe to fall, and she began to wish that he would say what he had to say and have done with it. But, again, he did not, and finally when the evening meal had been cleared, she could bear it no longer. She burst out with, ''Well? Why are you not badgering me?''

His eyes opened wide, but his lips twitched slightly before asking, ''Why ever should I wish to badger you, my sweet?''

''Oh!'' she cried. ''You know very well why. I should have thought that you would have been nagging me, long before this, upon the necessity for us to marry!''

''I never nag,'' he informed her calmly, but with a touch of humour in his eyes. ''And I have not mentioned it for the simple reason that I thought the matter already settled. We *shall* be married, you know. And I wish you would sit down."

He was seated comfortably in one of the fireside chairs, and she had jumped up to pace before him, but now she stopped to confront him. He had spoken with such irritatingly complete assurance that the level of her ire shot up by several degrees. However, as she observed his expression, she realized that in spite of his gentle smile, there was a rather implacable look in his eyes, and she thought better of giving free rein to her temper. Perhaps it would be wiser to remain unruffled and attempt to reason with him.

To give herself time to regain her composure, she stepped to the opposite chair, sat down and arranged her skirts carefully, then leaned towards him confidingly. Keeping her voice as quietly reasonable as possible, she said, "Charles, we are both agreed, I believe, that it is a most unfortunate situation we find ourselves in. I realize that there is no way in which we can prevent some scandal, for even if we were to marry there would be bound to be some malicious gossip about us. Society is made up of too many vicious people like Mrs. Parker. But what you must understand is that I care nothing for that. Oh! Not that I wouldn't prefer to do without it, of course, but— Well, what I mean to say is, if I were a younger woman, Melanie's age or even a little older, and desirous of finding a husband...but I am not. Or even if I were the type of person to whom Society and acceptance into the ton meant all, it would change the entire face of the thing. But I lead a very quiet life. I don't need balls and routs and all such vapid entertainments to keep me happy. So, you see, you are *not* obligated to marry me in order to save me from ruination."

He had listened to her without trying to interrupt, and with a promisingly interested expression on his face, but now he simply studied her own face, his expression a little puzzled. When he spoke, he surprised her by not referring directly to anything she had said, but by asking, "What *is* it that has you so adamantly against marriage?"

She was so taken aback by this question that it was a moment before she could answer. "Well...as I told you once before, I like my life very well as it is, and it would be no easy thing to change it all about at my age, and—"

"I wish you would stop harping on your age as if you were at your last prayers!" he interrupted.

She shook her head dismissively. "And, even more important, I like my freedom and independence far too much to marry and be obliged to give them up. Are you aware that marriage deprives a female of what few rights she has? Her money, her property, even her person and the very clothes on her back become her husband's to do with as he sees fit. I think it is an excessively high price to pay for having fallen in love." Her colour rose slightly before she added quickly, "And an even worse punishment if one is not in love."

Even in the midst of his astonishment, he felt a surge of hope and exaltation at her remark about falling in love. And he was encouraged to learn that it was not physical intimacy which she feared, but he put these things aside for later consideration. He, too, leaned forward, and said patiently, "No, I had never thought of that aspect of marriage. But, my dear, I am not an ogre, nor am I a particularly greedy man. I have no wish to deprive you of anything that is yours, and I promise you that as your husband, I shall do nothing which might concern you without your prior knowledge and complete agreement. If you like, I will put it in writing."

"Oh, that is not necessary. I trust you, but . . ."

"But?"

Her eyes slid away from his. He had completely disarmed her. Now was the time to tell him her true reason for refusing to marry, but she was so afraid that he would not understand, that he would look at her with contempt and loathing. And, confined as they were in this small inn, she would not be able to escape the awful unpleasantness which was sure to follow her revelation. She could not forget the look on his face when he had spoken of Melanie's possible ruination.

Misunderstanding her silence, he said, "Forgive me! I have not answered the other objections you have raised. In the first place, my dear, you say that you care nothing for the gossip which is certain to arise, but I don't believe that you have thought this through. Would it really leave you unmoved to be cut even by Bath Society, provincial though it may be? Oh, doubtless your friend Mrs. Gilbert would not *wish* to cut you, but she has a daughter of marriageable age whom she must establish. She cannot afford to be on friendly terms with someone of questionable reputation.

"Secondly, though you may not need balls, routs and vapid entertainments to keep you happy, surely a life devoid of not only those things, but of friends and acquaintances, with no one to talk with but your aunt Emily, cannot be regarded as happy. It would be a very lonely existence, Elizabeth."

At his words, she suddenly saw a lifetime of being shunned stretching out before her, with no one's companionship but Aunt Emily's. Dear, kind, maddening Aunt Emily, who neither understood her, nor shared her interests or her sense of humour. And, dear God! how could she have been so selfish as to forget Aunt Emily and what all this would mean to her? Her aunt would be even less able than she to bear the humiliation of being cut by their former friends and acquaintances.

The eyes she turned to Charles had such a dazed look in them that he was moved to exclaim, "Sweetheart! Don't look so tragic! You cannot deny that we find a great deal of pleasure in each other's company. And I promise you that I shall make you an exemplary husband. I want nothing so much as to make you happy.''

To her horror, tears welled up in her eyes and began to spill down her cheeks. Trying with little success to wipe them away, she choked as she exclaimed, "Oh! I *hate* women who are forever weeping!"

And as the tears continued to flow at an even more alarming rate, she cast him one anguished look, jumped up, and ran from the room, leaving Charles to stare after her in stunned perplexity.

CHAPTER TEN

ELIZABETH SPENT another nearly sleepless night, and though she was up quite early the following morning, she could not bring herself to leave her room before the noon hour. She was overcome with mortification each time she recalled her mawkish behaviour of the previous evening. She had been exactly like the sort of hysterical female she most detested! What must Charles have thought of her?

And when she was not remembering the embarrassing exhibition with which she had regaled him, she was sick with dread at the thought of having to tell Charles that she was not the innocent he thought her to be. The telling could not be put off much longer, for the snow had stopped sometime during the night, and it was entirely within the realm of possibility that they would be able to leave for Bath that very afternoon.

When Charles sent up a message by way of Alice, the maid, enquiring after her health, Elizabeth knew she had dallied long enough. She did not wish him to think her craven as well as hysterical, and so she stiffened her backbone, pasted a smile upon her lips and swept down the stairs and into the parlour.

"Charles," she said before he could speak, "I don't know when I have been so lazy. Please forgive my tardiness, and...and please forgive my ridiculous behaviour of last night. I can't imagine what came over me!"

His eyes quickly scanned her face with a penetrating look of concern. But when he could discern no evidence of illness, he relaxed.

"Oh, no need to beg my forgiveness," he said offhandedly. "I understand perfectly how it was. With all that has befallen you, a lesser female might very well have been thrown into strong convulsions!"

"Well, so I was," she answered meekly.

"No, no!" he teased. "I fancy yours was no more than a mild emotional frenzy. Don't let it cast you into despair! We shall speak of it no more."

And to show his good faith, he turned the subject. "The snow has stopped, you know, but I doubt we shall be able to set out before morning. In spite of the thaw, I've seen no vehicles pass by, so I can only assume the roads to be still impassable."

In fact, the first vehicle passed the inn later that afternoon, and Elizabeth knew that time was running out with a swiftness that was frightening. Though she held a book in her hands, and turned the pages periodically, she could not, if her life depended upon it, have said what she'd been reading. How would he take her confession? What would his reaction be?

So deeply engrossed was she in improvising various scenarios in which Charles was in some wonderfully understanding, and in others coldly condemnatory, that the sound of his voice startled her into jumping slightly.

"Now, what can you be thinking of with such very deep absorption? You have been staring off into space for at least the past five minutes!"

"I . . ." She faltered, knowing full well what she should say, but unable to make the words come. "I . . . was simply wool-gathering."

He stood abruptly. "What we need is a new diversion," he said decisively. "Shall I challenge you to a few rubbers of piquet?"

She eyed him thoughtfully, suddenly glimpsing a means of deliverance from a confrontation which, in her mind, grew ever more malignant with each postponement. Though she recognized that it was most probably a very foolish thing she planned, and one she was likely to regret in the near future, in her present state of mind it seemed the lesser of two evils. She was at the point where she thought she might attempt anything rather than lose Charles completely.

She agreed to the game with alacrity, and moved to the table where he was setting out playing cards, asking, "What stakes?"

"What is this?" he quizzed her. "Am I betrothed to a hardened gamester?"

"Hardly," she informed him, with more confidence than she felt, "for I only wager on certainties."

He raised an amused eyebrow. "A little too cocksure, my pet!"

"I think it only fair to warn you that I am very good. Papa taught me all he knew about cards!"

"Did he? Well, in that case, what stakes would you like?"

She hesitated, watching him deal the cards. "If I win—" she paused again, then rushed on before she could change her mind "—if I win, that you will agree that ours will be a marriage in name only."

His eyes met hers piercingly and his hands halted briefly before resuming their motion. "I see," he said somewhat shortly. "And if *I* win?"

"Oh, if you win, then you must name your own stakes."

"Fair enough," he replied ambiguously, taking up his hand.

It was decided that the winner must take two out of three rubbers, and the contest began in earnest. There was no bantering between them as the game progressed.

Elizabeth's belief in her infallibility was not mere boastfulness. Sir Jonathan had taught her well, to the point where he, no mean hand at cards himself, had seldom been able to best her. The game had scarcely begun, however, before she realized that Charles was proving to be a formidable opponent. In the ordinary way of things, this discovery would have done no more than increase her enjoyment of the competition, but in this case, it was essential that she win. To lose the contest would mean to lose Charles, for if he would not agree to a marriage of convenience, then she must make her past known to him. And there had never, really, been the slightest doubt in her mind as to what his response would be: after revulsion would come rejection.

They each won a rubber, but the games were very close, and unfortunately for Elizabeth, Charles had an uncanny ability to sum up her hands with disconcerting accuracy, as well as having the devil's own luck. Once the third rubber was begun, there was not the least question of the outcome. He won it in two swift hands.

His rather mocking smile caused her to say defensively, ''You might have warned me!''

''Your mistake, my love, was in taking me for a flat!''

''I did not, but...'' she shrugged slightly, hiding her chagrin and trying to tell herself that she had not had any real faith in so foolhardy a plan. ''Well, I must bow to your superior ability, I see. Shall we play another rubber?''

"It is growing late, and our dinner will be here shortly. But don't you wish to know what stakes I choose to claim?''

"Oh! Yes, of course," she said with as much unconcern as she could inject into her voice.

He said softly, "Our marriage, my dear, will be, in every way, a real one."

To her credit, she only blinked and inclined her head slightly, showing no sign of the sick turmoil she was feeling. In truth, she was filled with dread and did not afterwards know how she contrived to get through dinner with him with any degree of normalcy.

However, she did contrive, and after the table was cleared, Elizabeth went to stand by the fireplace, her back to Charles, while he poured them each a glass of wine. When he brought the glass to her, she took it distractedly and set it upon the mantel-shelf without tasting it. The moment had come for the dénouement. The time might be wrong, but she could think of no time that might be favourable for such an announcement. She only knew that she was making herself ill with the burden of holding it in.

Charles was standing at her side, one arm resting casually along the mantel, and she threw one quick glance at his face before turning her head away.

"Charles, I must tell you . . . that is, there is something you have a right to know. I . . ."

He said nothing, but simply waited patiently for her to continue.

She had rehearsed what she would say at least a thousand times, it seemed, but in the end none of those practised speeches came to her aid. To her horror, she heard herself blurt out the words baldly, with no pretty euphemisms to soften the telling. "I am not a virgin."

Though loud enough for him to hear, her voice came out very low, and she deplored the unsteadiness of it.

He remained completely silent as the seconds ticked by, until she, her nerves stretched taut, wanted to scream at him to say something—anything.

After an eternity, which in reality could have been no more than a few moments, he said quite calmly, "I see. So I have at last learned the secret behind your reluctance to marry."

"I am so sorry, Charles, but—"

"No doubt!" he interrupted her tersely. "May I ask . . . Good God! Not Braxton!"

"Certainly not!" she said with revulsion.

He gave a sharp bark of mirthless laughter. "Well, at least you show some taste."

"There is no call to be insulting," she told him indignantly. "What happened was not my fault."

His brows came together sharply and his whole body seemed to tense. "Were you taken against your will?"

Her eyes met his, then moved quickly away. She suddenly knew that if she could say that she had been taken by force, Charles would, in all probability, be able to accept her unchaste condition, and might even sympathize with her. But she knew, to her lasting regret, that it was not so. She had put up very little resistance that night, innocent fool that she had been, and as much as she would have liked to change that one damning fact, she could not. And she had never been a very good liar.

"No, don't lie!" he said harshly, as though he had read her mind, giving her no opportunity either to lie or to speak the truth. "Believe me, your face gives you away," he continued with a slight sneer. "So it was a seduction, then. May I ask who your lover was? Or should I say *is?*"

"Was—and he was *not* a lover!" she exclaimed.

"Who, then?" he demanded.

As though the words were dragged from her, she whispered, "I do not know who he was. I . . ."

"You allowed yourself to be seduced by a total stranger? How old were you?"

"Nineteen, but—"

"Nineteen! Certainly old enough to know what you were about," he said with contempt.

"If you would stop interrupting and allow me to explain..." she cried desperately.

"Spare me the sordid details!" he replied coldly.

Ignoring his scathing tone as much as she could, and attempting to remain as calm as possible, she said quietly, "I see that you are far too angry—"

Another humourless bark of laughter cut her off. "How very observant you are!"

Doggedly she persevered. "And it is obvious that there is no point in trying to reason with you now. You are in no mood to listen."

"I am not a gullible fool, and I can think of no plausible excuse which you could offer—but you may try!"

She lowered her eyes and shook her head slightly, knowing that nothing she might say would convince him or alleviate his anger.

"No? I thought not!" He stared hard at her, taking in her downcast eyes as well as the innocent-appearing blush on her cheeks, and was furious with himself for the strong attraction she could still exert over him. "My God! To think that I was considering you as the mother of my children, when you are nothing but a strumpet!"

She gasped, but he went on inexorably, "At least I suppose I ought to be grateful that you did not wait until I had married you before springing the truth on me! Damnation! When I think—" He broke off, slammed his fist down onto the mantel, then resumed in a quietly cold voice, "You will understand if I do not relish any more of your company tonight. Kindly be ready to leave early in the morning and do not keep me waiting."

Looking into his eyes, Elizabeth could see no trace of the warmth and humour she was used to finding there. They were now as cold and hard as his voice had been, and she wondered helplessly, and hopelessly, what had become of the man she thought she had come to love. Surely this angry, unbending stranger could not be he.

But, even in her distress, she recognized that further attempts at explanation, in the face of his determination not to hear any, could serve no purpose other than to leave herself open to more insults. Besides, she was dangerously close to tears once more, and she was resolved that he would not see her weep again.

With great dignity, and without saying another word, she turned and left the room. Surprisingly, she slept that night, but only after crying herself into that state of unconsciousness.

CHAPTER ELEVEN

IF THIS WAS LOVE, thought Elizabeth, as she dressed by the cold light of dawn the next morning, it was vastly over-rated and she was well out of it. The joys that had been hers since meeting Charles seemed scarcely to compensate for the misery she now felt.

She faced the dismal prospect of their return drive to Bath with as much dread as she had previously experienced when she had contemplated telling him of her fall from virtue. In point of fact, she felt almost faint from apprehension at the mere thought of enduring his animosity over the breakfast table, and she knew that if there were any other way of reaching Bath, other than in his company, she would have avoided him altogether. As it was, all she could do was try to console herself with the knowledge that once that ill-omened journey was accomplished, she need never see him again. Strangely, this assurance failed to bring her the comfort it should have.

Determined, despite her reluctance, that she would give him no opportunity to reproach her for the sin of unpunctuality, in addition to all else, she did not delay her descent to the parlour.

He was there, already having his breakfast, and did not bother to rise when she entered the room or even when she came to take her place at the table. That, as well as the one disdainful glance he flicked her way, was enough to convince her that his feelings towards her had not softened during the night. She gave a resigned sigh. So be it: she would not grovel to him, nor would she lower herself to beg for his leniency or understanding.

But his rudeness did not justify discourtesy on her part, and keeping her tone as pleasant as possible, she said, "Good morning."

He stared at her for a moment, his eyes like shards of ice, before saying with indifferent coolness, "Is it?"

Thankfully, his attention returned immediately to his plate, so he could not see how her face blanched at this evidence of his lack of regard for her. She barely suppressed a gasp of shock at the extent of his hostility and reached, with an unsteady hand, for a piece of toast. She did not trust herself to try for her cup for fear it would clatter or slosh, thus betraying her cowardly trembling.

She watched him covertly from beneath her lashes, saddened and somewhat bewildered that he could be so much changed, but she was forced to acknowledge, after a moment, that she really had not known him for so very long. Perhaps she had never truly known him at all; perhaps *this* was the real Charles, and the man she thought she had known was only a facade. If she could believe that, it would be easy to despise him as much as he despised her, for how could she care for a man who was such an implacable judge as to condemn her without a hearing?

But the sad truth was, as much as she wished to hate him, she could not. She could no more stop longing for one of his smiles, for that certain look of warmth in his eyes, or for one of his teasing comments, than she could stop breathing. There must have been something frightfully wrong with her to continue loving him this way.

If she could only meet his anger with her own, it might help to alleviate her unhappiness, but she hadn't even that consolation. How could she be angry, or blame him, when she felt such remorse over her own complicity in her seduction on that long-ago night? She had never, afterwards, understood what had happened to her then, but she knew that ladies were not supposed to enjoy that sort of thing. With such shame on her conscience, how could she not feel that he had a right to hold her in contempt?

Several minutes of strained silence had passed, and she knew that if they were to continue in close proximity for the next few hours, something must be done to ease the situation.

Taking a deep breath to bolster her courage, she said in a conciliating tone, "Charles, this will not do. I am more sorry than I can say for having been such a sad disappointment to you, but, much as I **might** wish it, I cannot alter the past. Neither can I alter the fact that we cannot be rid of each other's company for several hours yet. It would seem to me that the more comfortable course, for both of us, would be to try for a little more civility. Surely, sustained with the knowledge that you may be shed of me for all time once we reach Bath, you could manage just a trifle more amiability."

His eyebrows rose in exaggerated surprise. "Shed of you, Miss Ashton? You mistake the matter. Unfortunately, much as I might wish it, I cannot be shed of you so easily."

"I—what are you saying?"

"You do not always think things through, do you? But I have, and it has occurred to me that you have managed, quite successfully, to avoid exposing your sordid past in public. In the eyes of Society, your reputation is unblemished—up to this point. It is my misfortune that after this little escapade, Society will see *me* as the man who compromised you. And, being a gentleman, I am barred from disclosing the information that you were already most thoroughly compromised before ever I had the dubious pleasure of meeting you."

"You cannot mean that you still wish to marry me!" she exclaimed.

"It is not a matter of wishing. It is a matter of being constrained."

Elizabeth went quickly from stunned disbelief and hurt to deepest outrage. "Oh, no!" she cried. "I'd as lief be the world's most defiled pariah as marry you now!"

He shrugged indifferently, as though her wishes were of little importance to him. "I wish to leave here within the half hour. Will you be ready?"

"Certainly!"

Throwing her napkin upon the table, she rose abruptly and walked from the room as quickly as she could while still retaining a measure of dignity. But once in the hallway, with the door shut, she closed her eyes and leaned back against it, waiting for her tumultuous emotions to subside. She could not recall ever being so hurt and humiliated. Never in her entire life had she been treated so. And to think that she had several more hours of the same doubtful pleasure to look forward to! The thought made her stomach tighten painfully. How was she to endure it?

At that moment, Elizabeth became aware of a commotion on the stairs, and looked up to see Mr. and Mrs. Parker descending. They were attired in outdoor clothing, Mr. Parker hampered by several pieces of baggage, and Mrs. Parker issuing frequent sharp warnings interspersed with officious instructions for him. It was clear that they were preparing to depart from the inn, and Elizabeth pushed back more firmly against the parlour door so as to be out of their way.

While brushing past her, apparently oblivious to her presence, Mrs. Parker was saying querulously, "Were it not for your delaying our departure in the first place, Mr. Parker, we should have been comfortably fixed in Bath days since. But it is ever so with you! You think more of your confounded business than of *my* well-being. I only hope that we may not be on the road for hours longer than necessary, but I do not depend upon it!"

Elizabeth, hearing this, was seized with a sudden inspiration, and not allowing herself time to change her mind or to consider the folly of her action, she stepped quickly forward to say, "Excuse me, Mrs. Parker, but I wonder if I might ask a very great favour of you?"

A few minutes later, having collected her belongings and written a hasty note for Charles, she stepped into the Parkers' travelling coach. And only then, as it turned out of the inn yard and onto the road to Bath, did she begin to wonder if she had perhaps jumped out of the frying pan and into the fire.

CHAPTER TWELVE

IMMEDIATELY upon Elizabeth's leaving the parlour that morning, Charles had suffered a pang of conscience for his cavalier treatment of her. Her expressive eyes had been unable to disguise the hurt and shock he had caused her, and he had risen from the table almost as soon as she, his hand reaching out to her. But of course she had not seen that, and he had not been able to utter the words which could have halted her flight from the room, for in spite of his contrition, he could not wholly banish the anger that had taken strong possession of him. And one deplorable part of himself had felt glad that she was suffering as much as he.

Damn it! She had deceived him, and he had every right to feel betrayed—any man would. How could he have been so mistaken in his assessment of her character? He had thought her so perfect, when all the time she was no better than some and worse than many, and he had instinctively wanted to strike out at her, to retaliate for the bitter blow she had dealt him.

But he would not brood on that now. It would serve no useful purpose, and since they must go forward with this farce of a marriage, they would get over the heavy ground more lightly if they could, as she had said, behave civilly to one another. To be forever at daggers drawn would only make this affair more awkward and uncomfortable, and God knew it was already that.

So he had made up his mind that in future he would conduct himself with nothing less than scrupulous politeness towards Elizabeth. But then her note had been delivered, informing him that she had left with the Parkers, and all his good intentions had gone by the wayside. Of all the damned, mutton-headed things for her to have done!

A half hour later, he was tooling his curricle towards Bath at no more than a moderate pace—for he had no intention of overtaking the Parkers and thus rescuing Elizabeth—and occupying the time in devising ways in which he might, most effectively, point out to her the error of her latest start. He had just thought of a particularly incisive phrase, having to do with her want of discretion, when he came upon the Parkers' carriage, lying upon its side in the snow-covered ditch which bordered the road, and he pulled up shortly.

He knew, without the telling, that they had taken the curve here at too fast a pace for the condition of the road. In one comprehensive glance he took in the sight of the Parkers and their coachman hovering beside the overturned vehicle, but Elizabeth was not with them, and his heart immediately leapt into his throat as a picture of her, severely injured or dead, flashed into his mind.

In the next instant, however, he discovered her sitting calmly upon a fallen log at the other side of the road. This discovery, which should have afforded him the greatest relief, contrarily angered him beyond all reason, and his anger was only enhanced by the needless fright she had caused him. Never mind that it had not been intentional on her part; she was at fault for bolting with the Parkers in the first place.

Acutely conscious of the presence of others, he controlled his longing to give her a rare trimming, and as she stood and stepped towards him, he sprang down and handed her the reins. "Kindly hold the horses while I see if I can be of assistance over there," he said through gritted teeth.

Elizabeth took the reins from him without speaking and he strode across the road to confer with the Parkers, but it was only a matter of a few moments until he was back and handing her up into his curricle.

From the time immediately following the accident until Charles's appearance on the scene, Elizabeth had felt a not unpleasant apathy, once she had ascertained that she was uninjured except for feeling rather battered and bruised. But now a reaction was setting in, and Charles could feel the trembling in her hand as he assisted her up.

He waited until they were on their way, then asked gruffly, "Are you all right?"

"Yes, I am fine," she told him.

Subjecting her to a close scrutiny, he saw her give an involuntary shiver, and at the same time he detected an ugly bruise forming on her temple. The better part of his pique faded away in a rush of concern for her. "You are not!" he contradicted, and reached over to wrap the lap-robe more snugly about her legs.

"Thank you," she murmured, and after a pause, "What of the Parkers?"

"Their coachman will ride one of the carriage horses back to the inn for assistance."

He did not mention the fact that, owing to the delay that the accident would cause them, the Parkers had decided against going on to Bath. Let Elizabeth stew for a time, imagining the gossip they might stir up. She would be well served for showing such poor judgement as to run off with them. Though he would never have admitted it, his pride still smarted to think that she would prefer their company to his.

"Oh," said Elizabeth in answer to him.

They had been silent for several minutes when she said quietly, "I am sorry. I should not have gone off with them as I did."

"Well, why the devil did you?" he demanded, reminded of his grievances.

"Because you were being so damnably hateful! Oh, dear! There I go, losing my temper when I had only just promised myself I would not."

In spite of himself, a grin tugged at his mouth at this reminder of her unusual upbringing, and he cleared his throat loudly, resisting the unwelcome urge. "Yes, that's all very well, but I cannot, for the life of me, see how you could have thought it preferable to place yourself at the mercy of that tattle-mongering female. Your wits must have gone a-begging!"

"Very likely!" she said primly. "It is a pity that we cannot all be perfect."

"Well, we both know that you most certainly are not!" he was goaded into retorting, and was immediately sorry for it.

"Yes," she agreed in a hollow voice, and turned her head away, pretending to be absorbed in watching the passing scenery.

He muttered a curse, then said, "Forgive me, Elizabeth. As a matter of fact, I believe, as you do, that we must try for some civility in our dealings with each other."

Looking at him hopefully, she said, "Oh, yes! It will make this drive so much more bearable."

He glanced at her sharply. "I was not only speaking of this drive. I was speaking of our marriage, too."

Her eyes widened before she frowned, but when she spoke, her voice was perfectly amiable. "I don't know what maggot you have in your brain, Charles, but we are not going to be married."

He gave her one exasperated look, while her chin rose an inch or so into the air, and those were the last words spoken until they had nearly reached Bath.

"I gave you credit for more good sense than this," he remarked, as though there had been no break in their conversation. "You have no choice but to marry me."

"Oh, but I do! I have thought it all out, and have decided that if necessary, Aunt Emily and I shall remove to some place where I am not known."

He gave a short, derisive laugh, and said, "My foolish, green girl! Do you not know that there is no place you can go where gossip will not follow you, or even arrive before you? Do you intend to get rid of all your servants and hire new ones? Even then, I promise you, you would not be safe from the scandal-mongers!"

She felt a stab of dismay, but with every appearance of unconcern, replied, "Well, it is not your problem, so you may put it out of your mind with a clear conscience."

"Oh, yes! I daresay it would please you no end to see my reputation further blackened!"

"Gammon! It is common knowledge that no one cares a fig for how black a man's reputation may be!"

He threw her a fulminating look. "You would be well served if I washed my hands of you."

"Pray do!" was her rejoinder, but then she caught herself and said, penitently, "Oh, Charles, listen to us! We are at it again! Please believe me when I say that it would be the greatest mistake for you to marry me, feeling as you do."

He looked at her oddly, but as they had arrived in Upper Camden Place, he made no reply, and it was in a less than felicitous mood that they entered the drawing room a few moments later.

Aunt Emily and Lady Langley had heard the sounds of their arrival and were waiting, their expressions a peculiar mixture of fright, concern and guilt when Elizabeth and Charles walked into the room. The two women looked so like naughty children caught pilfering the cookie jar that without thought, Elizabeth's and Charles's eyes met, sharing the humour of the situation. But, suddenly becoming aware of what they were doing, they quickly looked away, and fixed their relatives with stern glares.

Both ladies appeared somewhat haggard; it had been a nerve-wracking week. Emily emitted a small yelp, and Lady Langley, who had spent every day in Upper Camden Place, worrying and praying, exclaimed, "Thank God, you are back! You can have no notion of what we have been through! My poor nerves are quite frazzled!"

Charles had moved to stand before his sister, and hands on hips, a sneer on his lips, he stared down at her. She cowered back into her chair as he said scathingly, "You've never had a frazzled nerve in your life! Stop prating nonsense about what you have been through and begin explaining yourself!"

"Really, Charles!" said her ladyship indignantly. "It was not my fault!"

"No, it was not her fault," echoed Emily.

"It was simply an unfortunate mistake," his sister informed him. "I completely misunderstood Melanie's note, and—only imagine!—she was spending the day with Lucinda the whole time!"

"An importunate mistake," breathed Emily.

The severity of Charles's expression had not lessened, and her ladyship hurried on, "Well, you can have no idea of our surprise when we realized what had happened. And who could guess that we would have that ghastly snow?"

"Yes, that ghastly snow," choked out Emily.

"Oh, for heaven's sake, Aunt Emily," cried Elizabeth irritably, "If you can do nothing but echo Lady Langley, then *do* just be quiet!"

Looking thoroughly cowed, Emily lapsed into silence.

"So," said Charles awfully, "you are going to brazen it out, are you? You aren't going to admit the fact that the two of you deliberately planned this whole business, eh?"

Emily moaned.

Lady Langley tried to look both haughty and hurt. "Charles! How can you think any such thing?"

"Easily! I only hope you are quite satisfied! Now all that is left for you to do is to convince Elizabeth that it is necessary for her to marry me!"

"Well, of course we are pleased that you recognize the necessity for a marriage. It is, after all, the only thing you can do, given the circumstances. It cuts me to the quick, however, to find that you suspect I would be pleased that you have been inadvertently placed in such . . . What did you say?"

"Yes," said her brother with perverse satisfaction, "I fancy that's thrown a spoke in your wheel. I am saying that Elizabeth is so ill-advised as to believe that our marriage is not essential. I have gone my length, trying to talk her round. I leave it to you to convince her, if you can." And turning on his heel, he strode out, saying, "I shall see you in Laura Place, Margaret."

Two pairs of eyes turned upon Elizabeth with a single look of fascinated horror.

CHAPTER THIRTEEN

"YOU NEEDN'T LOOK at me like that!" exclaimed Elizabeth, at once set on the defensive. "I have good and sufficient reasons for refusing to marry Charles—for refusing to marry at all!"

"Oh, Elizabeth!" wailed her aunt tearfully.

Lady Langley, who had made a fast recovery, smiled benignly and said, "Now, now, my dears. Such a great to-do over nothing. Do sit down, Elizabeth. I am sure you must be quite done up after that fatiguing drive." She waited until Elizabeth had reluctantly seated herself.

"Now then," said her ladyship in a tone to inspire confidence, "what is all this, about your not wishing to marry Charles?"

Elizabeth, becoming aware that she was nervously pleating the skirt of her gown, quickly smoothed it out, then clasped her hands tightly in her lap. "Well, ma'am, it has nothing to do with Charles. Indeed, I . . . I admire him greatly. But why must we be required to marry against our wishes when we have done nothing wrong?"

"My dear, would you so dislike being married to my brother?" asked Lady Langley, going straight to the heart of the matter.

"Oh, you do not understand!" cried Elizabeth.

"No, dear, I am afraid I do not."

Elizabeth sighed heavily. How to explain without divulging all? She had given Charles a disgust for her; she did not wish his sister to take her in strong dislike. And Aunt Emily would be certain to go off into violent hysterics. Strangely, it did not enter her head to doubt that Charles would keep her secret.

But she had other, equally valid grounds for refusing Charles's offer. She would concentrate on those. "Lady Langley," she said, her brow creased in her effort to make herself understood, "neither Charles nor I have ever wished for marriage. We have both found our lives quite comfortable as they are—or at least as they were," she interjected bitterly. "And now, because of a set of circumstances for which neither of us is to blame—" her frown became more pronounced as she recalled exactly who was to blame "—and in which neither of us have been guilty of the slightest transgression, well, it is . . . it is damned unfair!"

Aunt Emily gasped.

Lady Langley laughed delightedly. "Oh, my dear, forgive me, but I do find you so refreshing! But to answer your charge—you cannot be so innocent, Elizabeth. Good God! No one was ever promised that life would be fair! Just or not, it is the way of the world. Given a choice, Society will *always* believe the worst. No doubt it is a means of experiencing vicariously what they secretly long for themselves but are too chicken-livered to act upon. And you may be very sure that you shall be severely punished for their belief that you have enjoyed what they deny to themselves."

"Oh, I know that only too well, but there must be some way... I cannot allow Charles to immolate himself upon the pyre of my reputation!"

Not at all discouraged by this manifestation of concern for Charles, her ladyship declared, "Well, if that is all that is throwing a rub in your way, you may be easy. It is past time that Charles married, and it might just as well be to you as to another female. Better, in fact, for I am quite sure that he bears a fondness for you."

"No! I mean...oh! I cannot explain! But why? In God's name why did you do it?"

Lady Langley did not pretend to misunderstand, and she attempted to look apologetic. "Well, perhaps we should not have done, although it seemed a very good notion at the time." Then she added hearteningly, "However, what is done is done, but there is no need to fustigate over it now. My dear, you look worn to flinders. Why don't you go to your chamber and try to rest? Things are bound to look brighter when you are feeling more the thing."

Aunt Emily jumped up from her chair eagerly. "Oh, yes, dear. Let me take you up. A nice rest is *just* what you need!"

Lady Langley laid a restraining hand on her friend's arm and gave a small shake of her head. "I am sure Elizabeth can find her way on her own, Emily. You may see me to the door, for I really must be going."

"Oh!" said Emily uncertainly.

She looked at her friend questioningly, and her ladyship nodded reassuringly.

Elizabeth, having needed no persuasion, was already leaving the room, unaware of this little by-play, nor did she hear Lady Langley saying, a moment later, "Now then, Emily..."

IN THE SOLITUDE of her bedchamber, Elizabeth lay on her bed, staring up at the canopy over her head with unseeing eyes, while attempting to direct her thoughts into more constructive and less disordered channels. Feeling frustrated, angry and hopelessly dejected all at one and the same time, she was in no state of mind to argue her position rationally. How could she, when she was not at all sure of the rightness or wisdom of the stance she had taken? Perhaps she *should* give in and marry Charles. But, on the other hand, how could she allow Charles to martyr himself when he was in no way at fault?

And how could either of them find any happiness in such a marriage? Surely it would be torture to be tied to him as his wife, knowing he felt nothing but contempt for her. And yet, could anything equal the unbearable anguish of never seeing him again?

It brought a vague but very real physical pain to her chest—not unlike that she had felt when her father had died—to contemplate never again seeing Charles's warm smile, the way his eyes crinkled at the corners when he was amused, or the way he ran his fingers through his hair when he was irritated. How could she bear never again hearing the sound of his voice, his laughter or feeling the touch of his hand upon her arm, his finger against her cheek, his lips upon her forehead?

Oh, damn and blast! thought Elizabeth, angrily wiping at the tears on her face. She was becoming disgustingly maudlin, and it was getting her nowhere. If only she had never met Charles...but, no. Despite all, she could never regret having known him.

But she could and did regret the actions of her aunt and Lady Langley. If not for them, her life would not now be in such a shambles, and for a time, it made her feel somewhat better to give vent to her feelings by soundly abusing the two women in her mind. But only for a time. Though at present she resented having such a trait of character, she was too fair-minded not to give them credit for having good intentions. It was a pity that apparently no one had ever told them that the road to hell was paved with such things.

In the end, she stayed in her chamber for the remainder of the day, having a dinner tray sent up in the evening rather than descending to the dining room. If barricading herself in her room made her poor spirited, it could not be helped. At all events, she was still far too bitter over her aunt's interference in her life to confront her just yet.

By morning, though her thoughts were no less disordered, at least she felt enough in command of herself to face her aunt, and after they had finished a nearly silent breakfast together, she followed Emily into the morning room.

Aunt Emily immediately picked up her stitching and began working diligently upon it, looking the very picture of innocence.

"I must tell you, Aunt Emily," said Elizabeth with admirable composure, "that I find your behaviour in this affair to have been loathsome, deceitful, and . . . and traitorous! How *could* you?"

Her aunt's face twitched ludicrously as a series of diverse expressions flitted across it in her effort to hit upon the proper attitude to assume. While she still vacillated, Elizabeth spoke again, very softly. "Do not, pray, add to your list of iniquities by lying to me now and denying your culpability!"

Emily's face crumpled. "Oh, Elizabeth," she cried, "indeed, I did it for the best! I could not bear to think of you wasting your life away as an old maid! And, indeed, Charles seems so perfect for you in every way. I made sure you were not indiffident to him. Do not tell me you are, for I won't believe you. Indeed, I won't!"

"No, I shan't deny it, but that does not absolve you of guilt! You had no right to meddle!"

Emily sniffed piteously into her handkerchief.

Elizabeth shook her head sadly, despairing of ever being able to bring her aunt to a realization of her crimes. How she longed for a confidante: someone to whom she could pour out her story, and in return receive wise counsel, or at the very least, sympathy and understanding. But there was no one, only poor, inadequate Aunt Emily, who would be shocked and horrified were she to hear Elizabeth's dilemma.

"You really haven't a notion of what you have done, have you?" Elizabeth finally asked.

"I have only tried to ensure your future happiness!" declared her aunt stubbornly and defensively. "And for that, instead of thanks, I get nothing but recriminations!"

"No. I shall not thank you, for you have more likely ruined my life than otherwise! Whether you believe it or not, I have a very compelling reason for shunning marriage."

"Unnatural girl! I cannot, for the life of me, think what that reason may be! To be having these romansical notions about love is being foolish beyond perdition, and so I have told you these many years!"

"Well," said her niece with a sigh, "what is done is done, and to be arguing about it pays no toll. We must hope for the best, and perhaps it will not be so very bad, after all. I'm sure Wiggons will not spread the story, and we must hope none of the other servants will, either."

"Well, I pray you may be right," said her aunt doubtfully. "But these things always have a way of leaping out. I am sure I don't know how, but depend upon it, they do! And how we are to survive the scandal, if you will not marry Charles, I do not know, either!"

"Well," Elizabeth temporized, "let us not borrow trouble before we must."

BUT HER AUNT was proved right that very day. Aunt Emily had gone soon after their talk to spend the morning with Lady Langley, and when she returned later, pale and trembling, she collapsed into a chair, a hand clutched to her breast. "Oh, Elizabeth! It is all too true! Oh, I knew how it would be! Oh! Where is my vinaigrette?"

"Aunt Emily! What on earth?" Elizabeth knelt in front of her aunt, taking her hand and holding it between her own two.

Aunt Emily had leant her head against the back of her chair, her eyes closed, and now she peeked at her niece from beneath her lashes. "It is just as I said it would be—only worse. Oh, Elizabeth, the humiliation of it all! Margaret and I visited the Pump Room, and—oh, the nasty, sly smiles, and the whispers behind my back! I shall never be able to show my face again!"

"Oh, my dear! Was it so bad? I'm sorry, so sorry. But, listen to me, dearest. We shall leave Bath. We'll go to live in the country, or a small village, and you can have your own garden. You've always wanted a garden. You know you have!"

"Yes," said Aunt Emily pitifully. "But it will not be the same. I've grown quite fond of Bath...and the Pump Room, and my particular friends here. And I shall miss the concerts so. If only..." She trailed off.

"It will not be so dreadful, Aunt Emily. You will make new friends wherever we go. Remember how easily we adjusted to living here in Bath."

"But why can you not adjust to marriage with Charles?"

Elizabeth sighed. "Come, Aunt Emily. Let me help you to your room. We shall talk about it later when you have rested."

If more pressure than that had been needed to convince Elizabeth where her duty lay, it was brought to bear later that afternoon in the form of Lord Braxton.

When Wiggons announced that Lord Braxton had come to call, and was awaiting her in the drawing room, Elizabeth's first impulse was to deny herself to him. But that would have been craven, and so she went down to see him.

She entered the room to find him standing stiffly, facing the door, hands behind his back, and with a most stern expression upon his countenance. As she offered her hand to him, she said coolly, 'You wished to see me, my lord?''

He took her hand briefly. "Yes, Miss Ashton, I did," he replied, and began to pace about the room. After a moment, he continued, "Miss Ashton, I have been greatly distressed and unsettled in my mind. Last week I was severely shocked to observe you, with my own eyes, driving out of town with Mr. Carlyle, and with no chaperon to protect you and lend you countenance. I could only hope that you were merely going for a short drive with him, improper though that would be. However, I must tell you, such an explanation of your behaviour will not work with me. During the succeeding days, I called here no less than three times, and each time I was told that you were unable to receive me. No explanation was offered me, you understand, but I knew. Oh, yes, I knew. How could I not?''

He paused for a moment, but when there was no reaction from Elizabeth, he continued, "Well, not to wrap the matter in clean linen, there has been talk about you and Mr. Carlyle during the past few weeks. Not that I have wished to credit it. In fact, I did not, though I attempted to warn you about him. But what was I to think when I myself had the misfortune, once more, to witness your return to town in that same open carriage, with that same person, only yesterday?"

Here his voice shook with such strong emotion that he was forced to pause again in order to regain control of himself. Elizabeth merely watched him, too angry to trust herself to speak, and when he was able to, he said, "You may imagine, I am persuaded, into what perturbation I was thrown! I have made no secret of my admiration for you, Miss Ashton, and, indeed, I had quite made up my mind that you should be my wife. I had meant to come to you immediately, to confront you over this distasteful affair. However, I did not because my next impulse, of course, was to sever the connection cleanly! However, after a great deal of soul-searching, I have decided that I shall give you the benefit of the doubt, and assume that the worst did not happen."

"How very broadminded of you," murmured Elizabeth.

"Yes, but you will understand, I know, that it was no easy thing to overcome my very real scruples concerning this matter. It was only after a most fiercely fought battle with my better judgement that I was able to do so!"

"Indeed?"

"Indeed! A *most* fiercely fought battle! However, Miss Ashton, after long and deep contemplation, it is my belief that if you were to live quietly, and in perfect propriety—in a most exemplary manner—for the next year or two, the talk will die down, and then we may proceed with plans for our marriage."

"Sir, it is *my* belief that you are all about in your head! I have no intention of marrying you—now, in a year or two, or ever!"

"I am persuaded, Miss Ashton, that you are merely a trifle overset, and do not realize what you are saying. Therefore, I shall overlook it. Naturally, you do not like to think of waiting so long as a year or two for your happiness, but I do not see that it can be done any sooner. And, after all, you must know that you are not likely to receive a more advantageous offer."

She was so furious by then that she longed to strike him, but it gave her some satisfaction to see his shocked expression when she replied, "As for offers, my lord, I am pleased to tell you that I have received a *much* more advantageous one. I shall soon be wed to Mr. Carlyle!"

"You cannot wish to be married to that . . . that conscienceless rake!"

"On the contrary. I am quite sure that I shall like it excessively!"

He was horrified, and his mouth opened and closed ineffectually several times before he was able to say with rigid formality, "Miss Ashton, I have never been so shocked! Clearly I have been much mistaken in your character! I shall count myself fortunate to have been undeceived before it was too late!"

"I am in complete agreement with you, my lord. You can have no notion of how mistaken you have been!" Elizabeth told him. "But you were never in any danger, for I would not have had you under any circumstances! And now I think we have both said quite enough. I am persuaded that you had best leave before one of us is tempted to say something for which he may be sorry."

Without a word, he turned and left, and Elizabeth breathed a sigh of relief. She had finally sent her unwanted suitor to rout, and she thought of how Charles would laugh when she told him. But then, with a pang of regret, she remembered that she and Charles were not on such easy terms any longer.

She was leaving the drawing room when it suddenly dawned upon her that, without a thought, she had committed herself to marrying Charles. And somehow, in spite of all, it was like the lifting of a great burden from her shoulders to have the decision made.

CHAPTER FOURTEEN

AUNT EMILY, when apprised of the news later that afternoon, became almost crazed with delight and joy. Nothing must do but that a note must be sent round, instantly, to Laura Place, and when that was done, she plunged exuberantly into wedding plans.

"Of course you must wear your mother's wedding gown, for I have saved it all these many years for just this occasion, and of course you must have a trousseau. But for that, I am persuaded you will wish to have a London modiste, for you know, my love, that those here in Bath cannot compare. They are all very well in their way, but they will not do for your bride clothes. You will agree with me on that head, I know.

"Now, do let me think . . . oh, yes! We must have the imitations printed up, but of course, we cannot do that until we have made up a list of guests, and then, too, we must decide where it will take place. Do you not think St. George's in London, my love?"

Elizabeth, who had been wondering how Charles would receive the intelligence that she was now ready to accept his offer, had been listening to her aunt with only half an ear, but upon hearing Aunt Emily's final words, she looked at her aunt in appalled horror. "Good God, no! Aunt Emily, whatever are you about? These elaborate plans will not do. I will much prefer a very private, simple wedding here in Bath."

"Not St. George's?" asked Emily disappointedly. But her jubilation could not long remain suppressed, and she was soon bubbling over again. "Oh, well, I suppose Bath will do well enough. In truth, my love, the more I think on it, the better I like the notion. I am persuaded that it will be the most stumendous wedding Bath has ever seen.

"But I am forgetting. We must decide when it is to be. I fear it will take some time to arrange it all, but then, configuring all, perhaps it would be as well not to postpone it for *too* long a time. What do you think, my dear?"

"Forgive me, Aunt Emily. What did you say?"

"My dear, you are not listening, and I am persuaded that you should, for this is a very important occasion for you! One only gets married once, you know. Or, at least, one *should* only marry once. Of course if one happens to be a widow, or even a widower, one *may* marry more than once, however—"

"Oh, Aunt Emily! Stop! You are giving me the headache, and you may even be counting your chickens before they are hatched. For all we know, Charles may no longer wish to marry me."

Aunt Emily stared at her niece with astonishment. "Not wish to marry you? Have you run mad? Of course he will wish to marry you. He has no choice."

Elizabeth winced at this, but Aunt Emily was already pulling a sheet of writing paper from her desk and beginning to make a list, and so she did not see the result of her unwittingly tactless remark.

But Elizabeth was not so sanguine as her aunt, for she had begun plaguing herself with the possibility that Charles might no longer be of a mind to wed her. After all, she had refused him quite adamantly, had even invited him to wash his hands of her. Perhaps he had even left Bath, and at this thought, she felt a distinct sinking sensation.

But that fear, at least, was laid to rest when, shortly after dinner, Wiggons brought in a return note from Charles. Elizabeth opened it with trembling hands, and the sinking sensation returned as she read: "Elizabeth, Most gratified to receive your message. Will call upon you in the morning. Charles."

She stared at it despondently for several minutes, then castigated herself for being such a lackwit. What had she expected—a love letter? Not from a man making an unwilling sacrifice upon the altar of duty, certainly. And she had better keep that firmly in mind, else she was in danger of revealing her own feelings to him. And why that should be such a perilous prospect, she could not have said. She only knew that it would be, that such a revelation would somehow place her in a more vulnerable position than she already occupied, and that must be avoided at all costs.

WHEN CHARLES was announced the following morning, Elizabeth was certain that her thundering heartbeat must be clearly audible both to him and to her aunt, but he merely bent over her hand, murmuring politely, his countenance utterly impassive, before turning to Aunt Emily.

"Good morning, ma'am," he said with more warmth than he had shown towards Elizabeth.

"Oh, Charles. I collect you have come to discuss the wedding plans."

"As you say."

"Oh!" Aunt Emily's hands fluttered nervously, "Oh, yes! Oh, but, my dear boy, I must tell you—I am quite *aux angles!*"

Charles's eyebrows shot up. "Aux...?"

Elizabeth gave way to tension-relieving laughter, while her aunt gazed from one to the other in bewilderment.

"I believe Aunt Emily meant to say *aux anges.*"

"Well, I am perfectly sure that is what I *did* say!"

Two pairs of laughing eyes had met in perfect accord until Aunt Emily's voice brought them to a sense of where they were, and Elizabeth's face became a coolly polite mask, while Charles cleared his throat and assumed a faint scowl.

"Do sit down, Charles," Elizabeth invited him quietly.

"Thank you."

He seated himself, while Aunt Emily rang for refreshments, and the three of them discoursed upon the weather and the state of everyone's health with all the enthusiasm of mourners at a wake, until Wiggons had served them and withdrawn from the room.

Charles cleared his throat once more. "Margaret and I have discussed the situation from all sides, and have reached a solution which I believe will be best for all concerned.

"The two of you shall travel to Langley Hall within the next few days, in company with Margaret and Melanie, and we shall be married there, by special license. I shall leave for London today to procure the license and will join you at Langley at the end of the week." His dark brows lifted questioningly again at Elizabeth's look of dismay. "Have you some objection?"

Objection? Oh, yes! She objected most strenuously. She wished never to set foot in Langley Hall again for as long as she lived, but of course, she could not tell him that without disclosing her reasons, and that she was not prepared to do.

She said faintly, "I had thought a very private, very quiet wedding here in Bath would suffice."

"I agree that the quieter it is, the better it shall be. But you cannot wish to afford the Bath Quizzes more matter for gossip. The sooner you remove from this vicinity, the sooner talk will die down."

"Oh...yes, of course, but must it be Langley Hall?"

He frowned. "You have a preferable location in mind?"

She had not, and was obliged at last to admit as much, however reluctantly.

At this juncture, Aunt Emily suddenly stood, murmuring vaguely, "Oh, dear, I have only just remembered. I must speak with Cook." And with that, she fairly flew from the room.

Elizabeth could feel her cheeks burning with embarrassment at her aunt's transparent ruse and at finding herself alone with Charles, absurd as that was. Heaven knew they had been left alone together more often than not in the past, but his world-weary expression and the disgusted curl of his lips did not help matters any.

"I suppose," he drawled, "that one cannot wonder at your...fall from virtue, when one considers your deplorable upbringing. Of course, we are betrothed now, but I could have saved myself a deal of grief had I tumbled to your aunt's game early in our acquaintance, when she so constantly and improperly left us alone together."

"Charles ... please!"

"Oh, come now, my dear! If you think playing off these missish airs is pleasing to me, you couldn't be more wrong. At least grant me the consolation of deriving *some* benefit from your unusual rearing."

"Very well!" she said angrily. "I grant you that both my aunt and I were at fault, but if we are casting stones, then your sister must come in for her share. In fact, I would venture to say that she is due the lion's share, for I doubt very much that Aunt Emily devised that ramshackle plot!"

He inclined his head. "I daresay. At any rate, I concede the point."

"Thank you!"

"Not at all. Do you agree to travel to Langley as I requested?"

"I said as much."

"So you did. Then, if you have nothing further to say..." He looked a question.

"I..." She glanced away. "What of—what will happen after the wedding ceremony?"

"I shall take you to Brentwood, of course, before I..." He stopped and gazed at her for a moment, then asked abruptly, "How many?"

Her eyes met his, her brow creased in puzzlement. "How many?"

"How many men?" he asked shortly.

She was certain her face must be flaming now. "Only one, damn you! And only once!"

For a fleeting second, she could have sworn, a look of relief crossed his face, but it was gone instantly and he said softly, "Ah...a small blessing to be thankful for."

Knowing that it could only lead to further unpleasantness, but unable to stop herself, she challenged him. "How many women?"

He rose hastily from his chair, towering over her. "By God, woman! Have you no sense of what is fitting conduct in a lady?"

Determined not to be intimidated, she gave him stare for stare. "Perhaps I am more woman than lady!" she retorted and, ignoring his stunned expression, rushed on, "Oh, I am quite cognizant of the fact that ladies are not even supposed to be aware of the inevitable truth that men have numerous liaisons both before and during marriage. Or, at least, a lady is supposed to ignore that fact. And I know that the more women a man has, the more highly esteemed he becomes, whereas if a woman makes even one mistake she is held to be lower than the basest criminal! It is the greatest piece of bias! Who the devil made up such a rule?"

"Doubtlessly a man," he admitted, and was chagrined at having to suppress a strong urge to smile. This was no time for his damned, bizarre sense of humour to surface, and thank God she had lowered her eyes, so did not perceive his struggle.

Damn it! She was challenging one of man's most inculcated tenets, one it had never occurred to him to question.

He paced a few steps away, ran his fingers through his hair, then returned and lowered himself into his chair once more. "Listen to me, my dear. Inequitable as it appears to be at first glance, there is a very good basis for that particular rule. Oh, I am not saying that it is right that a man should . . . well, we shall not go into that just now. What I wish to say is that a man is expected to be experienced. It is to a bride's advantage that her husband have some experience." Then he added, in a bitter tone, "I am sure I need not explain that to *you!*"

Her eyes lowered swiftly again, and he sighed deeply. "Forgive me. I had not intended to rip up at you again. But to return to what I was saying . . . A female's virtue is the greatest gift she can give to her husband, and it should be saved for him alone, not . . . not given lightly and promiscuously to just any man who takes her fancy. Damn it, a lady is not supposed to feel . . ." He stopped himself again and frowned oddly before continuing. "In any event, aside from all that, there is an even more important, natural foundation for that rule. If a man's bride is not a virgin, how can he be certain that his children are his own?"

She had no answer for that. What could she say in her defence? That, except for that one fatal night, she had lived a totally blameless life? Even if that should count with Charles, she had no proof to offer him. Or, could she say that, despite her age at the time, she had been quite innocently unprepared for her will-shattering response to an unknown man's practised lovemaking? *That* was no excuse. A lady was not supposed to feel passion, and certainly not with a stranger.

She could recall, in surprising detail, the occasion when she had first learned that lesson. It had been one day during her twelfth summer, and she had come upon one of the housemaids and a footman in the home wood. They had been locked in an impassioned embrace, and she had been embarrassed by their obvious embarrassment when they had noticed her. But before that, she had been strongly impressed by their blatant enjoyment of the kiss they had shared.

She had gone at once in search of her papa to ask about this newly discovered aspect of the relationship between males and females, and would never forget his response to her naive questions. It was the first and only time in her memory when he had been truly uncomfortable with her. He had blustered and offered several vague explanations, but one thing had come through quite clearly: ladies of breeding did not experience such impure feelings as women of a lower order did.

No wonder Charles held her in contempt. He had every right, for she must be the most unnatural, the vilest of females.

She was startled when Charles reached out and took her hand, saying ruefully, "Elizabeth, how did we come to such blows? I promise you, I had no intention of doing so. In fact, I should like you to know that I am prepared to give you the benefit of the doubt, and shall endeavour never to throw your one mistake up to you again."

Elizabeth stiffened when his unfortunate turn of phrase reminded her of Lord Braxton's pomposity, and she came near to giving Charles a witheringly acerbic reply. But the urge only lasted for a moment. What a wretch she was! It was very good of him to be so magnanimous. She murmured a sincere "Thank you."

He squeezed her hand and smiled at her. "Well, then. I really must be going if I am to set out for London today."

She stood and walked with him to the door, where he turned and, placing a finger under her chin, lifted her face, then lightly touched her lips with his own in a light kiss.

"I shall see you in a few days' time at Langley Hall," he said, then looked as if he would say something more, but instead turned once more and was gone.

For a few moments after he had gone, she stood, transfixed, her fingers touching her lips in wonder.

Oh! He was so very, very good, and she so unworthy! But, despite the fact that she was quite undeserving, perhaps things would, after all, turn out right for them.

CHAPTER FIFTEEN

THE REMAINDER of that day and the following one were taken up with preparations for their removal to Langley Hall, and Elizabeth and Aunt Emily left early the next morning in Lady Langley's well-sprung, comfortable travelling coach. The ensuing trip might have proved tedious had it not been for Melanie's diverting chatter, as well as Lady Langley's interesting conversation, for which Elizabeth was most grateful. Little was said about the reason for their journey and, all in all, Elizabeth had little time for any worrying over her coming marriage and the problems likely to be attendant upon it.

However, her good fortune could not last forever, and that very first night, as Elizabeth prepared for bed, Aunt Emily paid her a visit in her bedchamber.

After exchanging a few pleasantries, her aunt hesitated and cleared her throat nervously. "My love, now that you will soon be a married lady, I feel that I must tell you a few things which you will have need of knowing. Not that I have had any experiments, but I did hear what Mama told Caroline—your own dear mama—on the brink of her marriage."

"Oh, no, Aunt Emily! You needn't!"

"But yes, my dear. I must! For you will have certain duties as a wife, you know, which, while they may not be quite pleasant, are none the less most important, and you must just design yourself to putting up with them. I mean that you must learn to accustom yourself to Charles's . . . to his baser desires, and try to bear with them with as much composure as possible. And you must always be amiable and compliant and, of course, never embarrass him with ill-bred questions or scenes if you should learn that he has formed a . . . a connection outside of marriage. For gentlemen, I understand, do have an unfortunate propendipity for that sort of thing, and really it means nothing, I have heard. It is just their way."

Elizabeth laughed. "Good God! It needed only that! I pray that you'll spare me, Aunt!"

"Well . . . but, Elizabeth, it is only what your own dear mama would tell you, were she here to give you advice!"

"Yes, my dear, and I thank you, but you've told me quite enough! You have done your duty, and now I am sure that you must be quite as tired as I, so I shall wish you good-night."

Elizabeth was gently pushing her aunt out the door of her chamber as she spoke, and when she was once more alone, she fell upon the bed in a fit of laughter. Surprisingly, she was so amused at the absurdity of her spinster aunt in the role of adviser to a new bride that she fell asleep rather easily with a smile on her lips.

SHE WOKE in the morning in the same light-hearted mood.

When she had dressed and gone down to the breakfast room, she found Lady Langley and Aunt Emily already there.

"Good morning, my dear," Lady Langley greeted her. "Did you sleep well? I think you must have done, for you look quite radiant this morning."

"Indeed, I did sleep well," said Elizabeth with a mischievous smile. "And that, in spite of Aunt Emily's grim portrayal of what I may expect as a married lady."

Lady Langley made an impatient sound in her throat and looked at her friend accusingly.

Goaded to self-defence, Aunt Emily said a trifle belligerently, "Well, but *someone* must have told her, and I *am* the nearest thing she has to a mama!"

"Good God, Emily! What a ridiculous ninny you are! What, pray, do you know of the matter?"

"Well, I do not, of course, but I have heard..."

"Humbug! The hearsay on that subject is so much rubbish! You would be better advised to listen to me, Elizabeth, for I know whereof I speak. That oft-repeated canard about ladies not being capable of enjoying certain aspects of married life is nothing more than a sham—a tale fabricated from whole cloth, and perpetrated by heaven knows who for God knows what purpose!''

"Do you mean . . . ?'' asked Elizabeth tentatively, scarcely daring to believe what Lady Langley seemed to be saying.

Her ladyship nodded her head emphatically. "I mean that with the right husband, a bride, lady or not, should be able to enjoy every facet of married life.''

Elizabeth would have liked to discuss this revolutionary notion further, but was prevented from doing so by Melanie's entrance into the room. In deference to Melanie's tender years and her unmarried state, conversation turned to her come-out, then to plans for the coming wedding.

What with one thing and another, it was not until later in the afternoon that Elizabeth found time to be private. When she was able to do so, without attracting unwanted company, she slipped out of the house to walk in the grounds, though she studiously avoided the summer house, while she examined more fully this new information which Lady Langley had presented her with. But, more important, she wished to think about what it meant to her.

It was difficult to credit. Heretofore, she had thought of herself as some sort of freakish creature, unfit to be called a lady, but if Lady Langley were to be believed, there was not the least thing wrong with

her. She was not an indecent wanton, and she needn't
be ashamed for having had feelings that were unnatural to a lady.

She paused in her walking and frowned, disturbed by a niggling impression that her logic was
faulty somehow, but unable, for a moment, to pin-
point the error of her thinking. And then it burst
upon her. Granted that such feelings might be natural and allowable, but they must still be prohibited to
an unmarried female. Her spirits sank to a new low.

What *was* the matter with her? Was she indeed a
wanton creature, incapable of controlling her baser
instincts when confronted by temptation? She
thought guiltily of her instant response those few
times when Charles had touched her, albeit quite in-
nocuously. But it could not be entirely so, for she had
been kissed, more than once, during her two Seasons, and those kisses, more ardent than anything
she had experienced with Charles, had done nothing
to arouse her; she had not even found them mildly
pleasing.

She could accept the fact that she reacted so
strongly to Charles. There was some excuse for that;
she was, after all, in love with him. But why in God's
name had she responded so to a stranger, a man she
could not even see in the darkness of that long-ago
summer night here at Langley? It was a question for
which she could find no acceptable answer, though

it festered in her mind through the afternoon and evening and long into the night.

NO ONE TOLD ELIZABETH, the next morning, that she looked radiant, and such an omission held no surprise for her. She felt positively hagged. Charles was expected to arrive sometime that day, and the wedding was to take place the following morning. She vacillated between excitement and dread, moping and irritation. It was unbelievably wearing and had a decidedly depressive effect upon her spirits.

Finally, after having spoken sharply to Aunt Emily twice in as many minutes, for which she was instantly sorry, she escaped the house and went to sit in the garden. But this time luck was not with her. Aunt Emily discovered her there just as she was beginning to feel a trifle more at ease.

Sitting down beside Elizabeth, Aunt Emily patted her niece's hand and said reassuringly, "Now, my love, you must not be frizzled. I am persuaded that it is nothing more than a case of bridal nerves, which cannot be wondered at. But are you not feeling cold sitting out here? I wonder that you do not take one of your books and go to the summer house, as you were used to do when we were last here. Do you remember, my dear?"

"Yes, Aunt Emily," Elizabeth sighed. "I do remember. But I would as lief not go to the summer-house just now."

"How very odd! For I am sure that you practically lived there the whole of the sennight we were here."

"Mmm," murmured Elizabeth, thinking that perhaps if she did not encourage conversation, her aunt would go and leave her in peace.

"It was such a lovely party, was it not, my love? It has been on my mind quite continuously since arriving here." Aunt Emily fell silent for a moment, presumably lost in recollections, but when Elizabeth said nothing, she continued, "It is a great pity, I think, that Margaret's scheme came to nothing."

Against her better judgement, Elizabeth asked, "What scheme?"

"Why, her scheme to make a match of it between you and Charles."

Elizabeth knew a sudden sense of alarm as she wondered fleetingly if perhaps her aunt's mind might be failing. She shot an oblique glance at Aunt Emily. "But, my dearest, her scheme did not fail. You cannot have forgotten that Charles and I are to be married."

Aunt Emily laughed delightedly. "Oh, Elizabeth, do not be absurd. Of course I have not forgot. It is my dearest wish come true. No, it was Margaret's *first* scheme of which I was speaking. That was to have taken place during the sennight we were here. Of course, I did not know of it at the time, for I only just learned of it quite recently."

Elizabeth turned towards her aunt. "Are you saying that Lady Langley had a similar plan to entrap me during that ridiculous house party? The same that we attended with Papa?"

"Well, of course, my love. There have been no others, for you know you have refused all such invitations for all these years, and you know my sediments upon *that* subject! But, indeed, Margaret was hoping to bring off a match between you and Charles at the time, though if it had come about, it would not have been at all the same! Indeed, it would have been perfectly proper, and not the havey-cavey business which it is now. And I must say that if it had come about, you would not have wasted all these years!"

"Very likely," remarked Elizabeth with a touch of impatience. "But you are forgetting that Charles was not here at the time."

"Oh, but indeed he was, my love. Only he did not arrive until late on the last evening of our stay, after you had retired for the night. And, if you will recall, we left very early the following morning, and so you never met and the whole of the plan was quite spoiled." She sighed heavily with regret.

"Charles was here, at Langley, on that night?" Elizabeth asked rather stupidly.

"Certainly, my love." Aunt Emily looked at her niece oddly. "Is that not what I said?"

Apparently Elizabeth answered appropriately, for Aunt Emily continued to chatter away, but her niece was no longer listening. She wished desperately to sort out her thoughts, but they were in a tangle of confusion, and Aunt Emily's voice kept intruding upon them, so that she was unable to carry any one of them to its conclusion.

Aunt Emily broke off in midsentence as her niece stood up abruptly and began moving away down the path. "But, Elizabeth," she cried in bewilderment, "wherever are you going?"

Elizabeth turned back to look at her aunt, as if surprised to see her there. "Oh! Aunt Emily! Forgive me, but I have decided that I should like to visit the summer house, after all."

"Shall I come with you, love?"

"Oh, no! Please don't, Aunt Emily. I would much prefer to be alone just now." And so saying, Elizabeth hurried away from her aunt.

Stepping into the summer house a moment later was eerily like going back in time for Elizabeth, and for the first time in all the intervening years, she allowed full play to her memories, with no attempt to block any of them. Once more, echoing through the recesses of her mind, she heard a husky, seductive male voice, and her fingertips remembered the touch of a firm, muscular chest....

On the few occasions when she had permitted herself to think at all of that night, one aspect had been especially distressful to her. It was bad enough to have been ravished, shameful to have actually enjoyed much of it, but when she thought that her ravisher was one of those elderly, married men who had been present at the house party, she had always felt faintly ill.

Now, as she stood in the middle of the small enclosure, gazing at the chaise where it had all taken place, she wondered how she could ever have thought for a moment that such a thing could be true. It could not have been any of those men. But if Charles had truly been here that night... In a sudden flash she *knew*, and without the least trace of doubt, that her seducer had been Charles himself.

It was difficult to take in all the implications of such a momentous discovery, and for a moment, the enormity of it stunned her. Then an overwhelming relief made her feel light-headed, so that she found it necessary to brace her fingertips against the small table beside her. Although she did not attempt to consider why, the thought that it had been Charles comforted her.

But gradually other memories began to trespass upon her wandering thoughts. What was it he had said that night? *Forgive me. I thought you were someone else.* The words came back to her as though it were yesterday, and she suddenly remembered the exceptionally attractive Lady Sabina. Oh, yes, she thought, with the beginnings of resentment, no doubt he *had* thought her to be someone else! He had thought he was making love to another woman, and here she stood, like an idiot, feeling gratitude for what he had done.

Disgust with herself as well as anger towards Charles grew rapidly as she recalled how he had insulted her, humiliated her, at the inn upon learning of her past. And when she thought of the past few days, of how unworthy she had felt, and how grateful towards Charles, she cringed inwardly. This man, this rakehellish villain, for whom she had been feeling such maudlin tenderness only moments before, had ruined her, then scorned her for having been his victim. And as if that weren't enough, he had then been so high-minded—so very *generous*—as to be willing to marry her, in spite of her depraved character. Well, she would see about that!

A slight noise made Elizabeth jerk her head round towards the doorway. As if conjured up by her thoughts, Charles stood there, glancing curiously round the room before bringing his eyes back to meet hers.

With one of his most disarming smiles, he said softly, "Hello, my love."

"You!" Elizabeth exclaimed in tones of revulsion. "You vile, loathsome despoiler of women! You—you damned libertine!"

CHAPTER SIXTEEN

CHARLES STARED at Elizabeth in utter astonishment. Now what the deuce had her flying into the boughs? Had she got some maggot in her brain, imagining that he'd been playing fast and loose while in London? He was stung by the injustice of that supposed, but erroneous, criticism, and his brows snapped together in a scowl. He was all the more indignant when he recalled how he'd scarcely been able to think of anything but her for the whole of the time he'd been gone.

"What the devil?" he demanded, taking a step inside the doorway.

As he did so, Elizabeth retreated a step, raising her hand in a gesture to ward him off. "Do not come near me!" she snapped.

"Oh, confound it!" he ejaculated, ignoring her warning and moving closer. "I wish you would stop these high dramatics!"

But as he made as though to take hold of her, she drew farther back, out of his reach. "No!" she cried. "Don't touch me! Don't ever touch me again!"

"Damnation!" he growled, his arms dropping to his sides. "What the devil is the matter with you?"

"As if you didn't know!" she retorted, then added, "No! Very likely you do not know, for I am quite sure that you have ravished any number of unwilling females in your long career as a rake!"

He ran his fingers through his hair. "I wish I had some notion of what you are talking about. I will tell you, however, that you are labouring under a mistaken belief if you think that I have ever ravished any female, unwilling or otherwise. I will admit, however, that I have seduced a few." His evil genius caused him to add, "And you are even more wide of the mark if you think any of them were unwilling."

The absurdity of this disputation had suddenly struck him, and he had made the last remark half in jest. After all, she had been aware of his reputation from the start. A grin tugged at his mouth. Surely she could see how asinine this conversation was! But obviously she could not. She seemed more incensed than placated by his poor attempt to inject some humour into the situation.

"Oh, how like you!" she accused. "Well, *you* may find it quite laughable, but I assure you, *I* do not!"

He sighed. "And possibly I would not either, if I only knew what it is that has put you into such a taking. If you are accusing me of having seduced one or more females while in London, I can tell you, my girl, you are dead wrong!"

"No, and I would not care a jot if you worked your libertine wiles on the entire female population of London! There is only one female who concerns me, and that is myself!"

Charles was so thrown off his stride by this statement that for a moment he could only stare again, but finally he said, "One of us is mad! If I have seduced you, I promise you, *I* know nothing about it!"

"No? Well, perhaps I can jog your memory a bit by telling you that I was a guest here at a certain house party several years ago. I was nineteen years of age at the time."

A wary expression came into his eyes, but he said nothing, so Elizabeth continued. "Is your memory still in need of a nudge? How will it be if I tell you also that this is the second time in my life that I have found myself alone with you in this summer house?"

"Oh, my God!" he muttered, full realization dawning. "It was you?"

She averted her face. "Yes, damn you!"

"Elizabeth..." His voice held an odd note, compounded of remorse and pleading, but she was too overset to hear it. He lifted his arms halfway towards her, then dropped them once more as she stiffened. "What can I say? I am sorry for it. Lord, I was sorry that night, but you ran away so quickly and I could not discover who you were. I was not even aware that you had been here."

"And *that* is supposed to excuse you?"

"No, of course not, but if you are implying that I am wholly to blame, that is a cock that won't fight! What the devil were you doing out here in the middle of the night?"

This home thrust did nothing to soothe Elizabeth's overwrought state. "Oh, yes! Ease your conscience by shifting the burden of guilt to my shoulders! I had merely come out of doors for a breath of cooler air that night. How was I to know that I would not be safe here? Ignorant, green fool that I was!"

"No, I don't mean to exonerate myself, however—" He stopped himself before he could blunder into worse quagmires. "Well, this is nothing to the purpose. At least I can now make reparation for the wrong I did you."

Elizabeth said stiffly, "If you are referring to your offer of marriage, sir, it is now quite out of the question. I cannot marry the man who has ruined my life."

Having rid herself of so much spleen, she should have been the happiest of creatures, buoyed up with a righteous sense of vindication. She had struck a blow in retaliation for the great wrong he had done her. But perversely, she had begun to feel lower and lower with each spiteful remark, hating herself for taking such petty revenge, but somehow unable to stop herself.

Why could he not see how very miserable she was? Why did he not sense how she longed for him to overcome her silly, prideful rebuffs? If he cared for her at all, he would now take her in his arms, despite her foolish objections, and convince her that he truly wished to marry her, that everything would come right for them.

But he did not. Instead, he turned away to stand in the open doorway, one hand braced against the door frame, and a pregnant silence stretched between them.

How could he tell her, now, that he loved her? That he had come to terms with her lack of virginity while in London, and that it mattered not a whit to him? He could not deny that he had been overjoyed to realize that he had been her only lover, that she was the mysterious love he had never been wholly able to banish from his memory or his dreams. But would she believe him if he were to tell her that it would have been of no consequence to him if it *had* been another man? That she had not been out of his thoughts for more than a few minutes for the entire time he was away? That he had come to feel that they were two halves of a whole and that a part of him was missing when he was not with her?

No, he thought not. She was more likely to laugh in his face, and who could blame her? After his damnable jealousy and stupid, ingrained male pride had caused him to behave like some cursed, stiff-necked prig while at the inn, she must loathe him with a vengeance.

He sighed deeply. It seemed to him that the only honourable thing to do, if he wished for her happiness, was to give her the freedom she so desired along with the assurance that her reputation would still be intact.

Without turning to face her, he said quietly, "Certainly, if it is what you wish, I shall not attempt to force you into an unwanted marriage. And you will be glad to know that your reputation has not been damaged by our sojourn at the inn. There has been no talk. Apparently the Parkers had a change of mind about going to Bath, and Margaret had let it be known, while we were away, that I had merely escorted you to stay with a sick friend. Fortunately, Margaret possesses the three attributes most esteemed by the ton—birth, rank and fortune—so you need not fear that her word was not accepted."

"But—" Elizabeth bit her lip to keep from blurting out that he was *wrong!* That she wished to marry him more than anything on earth, and that her damned freedom meant nothing to her without him. But what a mistake it would be to tell him so when it must be the last thing he would wish to hear. Not when he must have felt such relief at being freed of any obligation to her. After all, if he had wanted her, he would not have given up so easily.

He mistook the direction of her thoughts. "Oh, I know what your aunt told you. I'm sorry to say that our relatives have been meddling again. The visit to the Pump Room, the whispers and looks that so humiliated your aunt were all products of their overly fertile imaginations."

She had to blink rapidly and swallow the awful lump in her throat before she could say, with a semblance of normalcy, "I see."

He turned back into the room and smiled, but she quickly averted her eyes to hide the tell-tale moisture in them, and did not see the bleakness in his own eyes. He said a little gruffly, "I wish you happy in your future life, my dear. But I would make one suggestion, if I may."

"What is that?" Her voice was barely above a whisper.

"Since our betrothal is of so recent origin, it might look better if you were to wait a decent period of time before crying off."

"Yes . . . certainly."

Both stood there as though waiting for something that did not happen, until Elizabeth could bear no more. If she did not leave him, this very minute, she would surely shame herself and embarrass him by throwing herself at him and begging him to have her. Slipping past him, she gasped, "I must go!"

Charles watched her until she was out of sight, then slammed his fist against the door frame, and cursed fluently at himself.

It did not help.

CHAPTER SEVENTEEN

ELIZABETH SAT in one corner of the travelling chaise, staring listlessly out the window while her mind replayed, yet again, that devastating scene with Charles in the summer house at Langley. Why had she done it? Why had she driven him off with her stupid, pettish temper? She had foolishly allowed her wounded feelings and lacerated pride to betray her into saying things she had not meant, and now Charles was lost to her forever.

If only she could take back the angry words. If only Charles had arrived later after she had had time to put things into proper perspective. If only Charles had seen through her idiotish behaviour... if only Charles could love her.

She leaned her head wearily against the back of the seat and closed her eyes. Not all the "if onlys" in the world could change one second of what had taken place. She could not take back the words; Charles had in fact arrived on the tail of her shattering discovery; he had not seen through her behaviour, and most painful of all, he did not love her.

She fought back a fresh onset of tears. Lord, one would think they would dry up eventually, but she seemed to have an endless supply. She must stop reliving the past, for it was so damnably futile. But no sooner did she tell herself this than her thoughts reverted to the previous day: surely the most wretched day of her life.

The drama that had taken place in the evening was nearly as difficult, in its own way, as the earlier one with Charles. Elizabeth shuddered to recall how her aunt had received the news that her niece meant to cry off from the engagement and return to Bath the next day. At first unable to do more than utter a series of disjointed and disbelieving ejaculations and phrases, Aunt Emily was soon brought to the unwelcome recognition that Elizabeth was perfectly serious.

She had burst into a fit of weeping and cried, "Oh, you wicked, unnatural girl! I had never subjected that you could be so selfish! Oh, to have come so close to having my dearest hopes realized, only to have them deployed in such a way! It is too much! You cannot be so cruel! You must tell Charles you are sorry for whatever it is you have said to him!"

"Oh, Aunt Emily, I promise you I would if— But, indeed, I cannot."

"And, pray, why can you not?" Aunt Emily demanded. When Elizabeth could only shake her head sadly, she declared, "Oh, you are sharper than a servant's tooth! Have you no thought for your reputation? In addition to all else, you will be known as a jilt. And what of my feelings? Have you no care for those?''

Elizabeth could do no more than assure her aunt of how very sorry she was, something she was aware of having been obliged to say far too often lately. But Aunt Emily was in no frame of mind to accept her apologies, and in the end asserted that she wanted nothing more to do with a girl so depraved and freakish as to whistle such an advantageous alliance down the wind. She refused point-blank to accompany Elizabeth to Bath.

Lady Langley, surprisingly, had had little to say but in fact had been all that was kind and considerate.

Charles she had not seen since leaving the summer house, for he had sent a message excusing himself from dinner and had not appeared by the time Elizabeth escaped to bed. Nor had he been anywhere in evidence that morning when she had left Langley Hall with only Jennings to keep her company.

Well, it was over, she told herself, wiping the tears away resolutely, her chin rising with determination. There was nothing for it but to get on with her life, and to keep herself so busy that she would have no time to indulge in these morbid repinings. She would throw herself into redecorating the house in Bath, and when that was done, perhaps she would try her hand at writing. She had always wanted to do that. And, in time, the dull ache which seemed to be permanently lodged in her chest would go away along with the bouts of acute anguish which sometimes overcame her when her memories became too poignant. But even as she thought it, a new wave of despair swept through her at the thought that she would never again share a joke with him, and would most likely never even see him again.

Elizabeth was pulled up from the depths of her misery by the sudden slowing of the coach, which then drew to a lurching halt. As she exchanged questioning looks with Jennings, who sat across from her, she became aware of rapidly approaching hoofbeats.

"Oh, miss," squealed Jennings fearfully, "'tis a highwayman, for certain. We shall be robbed, and very likely killed with no proper escort to protect us!"

"Nonsense, Jennings! There is very little an escort could do against a determined highwayman, and we shall not be killed. He will be after our valuables, not our lives. Do get hold of yourself!"

"Well, I hope you may be right, Miss Elizabeth, but there is worse things than being killed," muttered Jennings darkly.

Elizabeth flashed her maid one exasperated glance before turning her attention to the rider who had pulled up beside the coach. Her own heartbeat settled to a more normal rhythm as she took in the fact that the man wore no mask, and was pulling his forelock deferentially. Elizabeth lowered the window.

Leaning down to peer at her through the opening, the man gasped, "I'm come from Langley Hall, miss, wi' a message from 'er ladyship. Yer to turn back, if it please yer, miss. It's yer aunt. She's been taken right poorly and they've 'ad to send fer the doctor."

Elizabeth's face paled, but she did not give in to the terrible fear which clutched at her heart. "You must ride back quickly, and tell her ladyship that I shall be there as soon as possible," she instructed the rider.

As he galloped away in the direction from which he had come, Elizabeth calmly directed the coachman to turn about and return to Langley with all speed. She then turned to her blubbering maid, admonishing her to put a damper on her overwrought sensibilities.

Only when all this was accomplished did she allow her own apprehensions to take possession of her mind. What had she done? What if Aunt Emily had suffered a fatal attack because of her selfish pride? How would she be able to forgive herself for such a thing? Oh, pray God she would not arrive too late!

Almost ill with fright and worry, Elizabeth scarcely waited for the carriage to come to a full stop at Langley Hall before she jumped down, unassisted, and ran up the steps. The doors opened before she reached them and Charles stood there, and it seemed the most natural thing in the world to take the hands he held out to her, and allow him to draw her into his arms.

"Sweetheart," he soothed, "do not look so distressed. It will be all right, I promise you. Your aunt is resting comfortably and the doctor will be here shortly. Come and sit down while I get you a glass of brandy."

She raised her head from where it had been resting against his chest, her frightened eyes scanning his as she clutched the lapels of his coat. "Oh, no, Charles. I must go to her at once!"

"In a moment, love. I assure you, she is quite comfortable at present."

Charles's voice was husky with the effort it cost him not to kiss the delectable mouth so close to his own, but an uneasy guilt lent aid to his powers of resistance, and instead, he led her to the library and assisted her into a chair.

As he went to pour some brandy for her, she asked anxiously, "Will she be all right, Charles? Please, you must not attempt to spare me. You must tell me the truth."

"My darling, I give you my word, she shall recover. I am sure of it. Now, drink this and compose yourself. You will not wish her to see that you are so overset."

"No, of course not," she murmured, taking a sip of the dark liquid and coughing a little as it burned its way down her throat.

Somehow, just having Charles near was immeasurably comforting and that, along with the brandy, soon made her feel more hopeful and relaxed. Becoming aware that she had not even removed her bonnet and pelisse, she did so, then smiled at Charles. "I am feeling much more the thing now and should like to see Aunt Emily if I may."

"Certainly, my sweet. Come along and I shall take you up to her."

Elizabeth felt another shock of fear as she stood at her aunt's bedside. The curtains at the window were drawn and there was only one branch of candles burning in the chamber, but even in that dim light, she could see the unnatural pallor of Aunt Emily's complexion, and the hand she took in her own was alarmingly cold.

Aunt Emily's eyes opened and she smiled faintly. "You have come," she whispered in a thready voice. "I knew you would, my love. You are a good girl, and I should not have lost my temper with you."

"No, no, Aunt Emily. It was all my fault. But you must not try to speak. You must rest and regain your strength, my dear."

"So good to me," whispered Aunt Emily, closing her eyes once more.

Elizabeth's hand went to her mouth as she turned her apprehensive gaze towards Charles.

He looked nearly as disturbed, and shot a sudden look, which seemed strangely angry, at his sister, who stood at the other side of the bed. He opened his mouth to speak, but was forestalled when Lady Langley declared, "I believe I hear the doctor now!"

The door opened and a rotund little gentleman, carrying a small black bag, bustled officiously into the chamber. "Well, well," he said, approaching the bed as Elizabeth and Charles stepped back to make room for him, "What have we here?"

When Lady Langley had described Aunt Emily's symptoms to him, he nodded his head wisely, said, "Hmmmmm," then demanded that the room be cleared of all but her ladyship so that he could get on with his examination.

Elizabeth's objections to being excluded were soon overcome, and Charles led her from the room after telling his sister, rather sternly, that he wished to see her in the library when she was free. He then escorted Elizabeth to her chamber, advising her to rest and promising that she would be called and could speak with the doctor as soon as he finished ministering to her aunt.

The waiting was an agony for Elizabeth who, unable to rest, spent the time pacing in her chamber. But finally she was summoned to the hallway outside her aunt's door, where the doctor awaited her.

"Shall she recover, doctor?" Elizabeth asked pleadingly.

"Oh, yes," replied the doctor, "I have every expectation that she shall, so long as she is kept quiet and not allowed to become agitated over anything. If that should happen, I can guarantee nothing."

"Oh, you needn't fear. I shall allow nothing to overset her, I promise you."

"Good, good!" responded the doctor. "I have left a draught with her ladyship to ensure that the patient gets plenty of rest, and I shall call again tomorrow to see how she does."

As soon as the doctor had gone, Elizabeth hurried back to her aunt's bedside, where she spent the remainder of the afternoon until dinnertime, watching Aunt Emily sleep. At both Lady Langley and Charles's insistence, she did leave her aunt long enough to go down for dinner, but was back again as soon as the meal was over, and would have stayed for the entire night had not Charles assured her that either he or Margaret would be with her aunt the whole time. Even then, she might not have allowed herself to be persuaded had she not been so exhausted, both emotionally and physically, and had Charles not pointed out that with the medication supplied by the doctor Aunt Emily would very likely sleep soundly throughout the night.

It was not until Elizabeth was in bed, mentally reviewing the events of the day, that it occurred to her to wonder at Charles's attitude towards her since her return. It struck her, in retrospect, that he had been rather warmer than one might have expected, given all that had gone before. Had he not used several endearments when speaking to her? Yes, definitely he had. But what did it mean?

She shook her head irritably. She must not fall into the error of thinking that it meant more than it actually did. After all, he was an accomplished and practised flirt, and endearments had always come easily to his lips. And yet, the ones he had employed today had seemed subtly different from those he had used when first they met. The way he had spoken to her today, the tenderness she thought she had glimpsed in his eyes, the caring concern he had shown her did not seem to betoken mere flirtatiousness.

But no! It would be much wiser not to think along such lines. He was simply being kind, offering friendship and support in a difficult situation, and she must be grateful for that and not ask or wish for more. It would be the height of idiocy to begin imagining that he harboured sentiments that did not exist. It would be foolish beyond permission to do so, tantamount to self-flagellation on her part. She must not be such a silly goose as to open herself to the pain of rejection once more.

But despite her resolution to put a strong guard upon it, she could not prevent her ridiculous heart from swelling a little with hope.

While Elizabeth was thus occupied, Charles stood stiffly, hands clenched at his sides, facing his sister across the width of Aunt Emily's bed. "Damn it, Margaret! I tell you, I do not believe I can go through with this! I must have been mad to have agreed to such outrageous chicanery. Lord, never in my wildest imaginings did I ever think that I might one day fall in with any of your cunning machinations!"

Aunt Emily, propped up against the headboard with a profusion of pillows behind her, turned her worried eyes from Charles to her friend as Lady Langley straightened from where she had been diligently cleaning the layer of pallid *maquillage* from Emily's face.

Lady Langley cast a look of disgust at her brother. "Good God, Charles! This is no time to come over all righteous! You had no such scruples last night when you agreed to this, and it is working beautifully, you must admit. What do you imagine Elizabeth will do if she discovers how we have tricked her before you have had time to win her over? If you think she will remain here in such an event, you are a great nodcock! I wish I may see it! She would leave on the instant and you would be thrown into flat despair again. How else do you propose to keep her here, pray?''

Charles threw himself into the bedside chair. ''Confound it all, I don't know! But I had not considered how frightened she would be, and I cannot bear to see her so.''

'''Tis very handsome of you, but I had not thought you to be so pigeon-hearted. You are making a great piece of work over nothing! There is not the least occasion for this nonsensical flight of yours. Elizabeth is not such a frail creature and, in any case, by tomorrow we shall allow Emily to seem much improved. I shall apply a much thinner coat of face paint and on the next day we may not need to use it at all.''

Charles glanced at Emily's face with distaste. ''Where the devil did you come by that disgusting stuff, anyhow?''

''Oh,'' said Lady Langley, bending to her task once more, ''we were used to have frequent amateur theatricals here. They were all the rage, you know. And what a fortunate thing it is that I saved this 'disgusting stuff,' but I always knew that I would one day find a good use for it.''

Charles watched the operation in brooding silence for a moment, then asked, ''And what do you suppose will happen if Miss Godwin should forget herself and slip out of character at some point in this charade?''

"You must call me Aunt Emily, dear boy!" twittered that lady.

"Oh, I think there is not the slightest danger of such an occurrence," his sister told him confidently. "It cannot have escaped your notice that Emily has a most amazing talent for acting. I do believe she might have had a career on the stage, had she so desired."

Aunt Emily blushed with pleasure. "Indeed, I do think I did quite well, did I not? And truly, it has been rather diversing, though it is a trifle wearing to pretend to be sleeping for such lengths of time, and I *do* hope I shan't be obliged to plunge my hands into that freezing water too often."

"No, no! I do not think that will be necessary again," her friend assured her.

"Good Lord!" Charles groaned. "I do not believe this! You are both bedlamites, and I have allied myself with you! If Elizabeth should ever discover this, I would not wager a groat on my chances of winning her!"

"Then you had better work quickly, and bring her to hand before she does discover it, had you not?"

Charles only groaned again.

CHAPTER EIGHTEEN

IN THE MORNING, Elizabeth visited Aunt Emily before going down to break her fast, and was pleased to find her aunt seemingly improved. She still seemed more weak than Elizabeth could like, but her colouring, while not yet natural, appeared less pallid than on the previous day, though it was difficult to be sure in the subdued light of the room. However, when her niece suggested that the drapes be opened, Aunt Emily became so agitated that Elizabeth did not insist.

The physician arrived soon after breakfast and was shortly closeted in the bedchamber with Aunt Emily and Lady Langley, and once again Elizabeth was excluded. But though she resented this banishment, she accepted it without demur when the doctor quietly reminded her that Aunt Emily must not be overset.

And, indeed, she soon got over her pique when Charles appeared, saying, "Come along, my dear. You must leave the good doctor to work his miracles as he sees fit. I am going to introduce you to my ancestors."

Without allowing her the opportunity to object, he drew her hand through the crook of his arm and led her to the main wing of the house where the portrait gallery was to be found. Stopping before the first of these, a man who had every appearance of being a rogue, Charles said, "Here you see the gentleman whose namesake I am, Sir Charles Carlyle, the founder of my family. What do you think of him?"

With the devilish gleam in the eyes of Sir Charles's likeness fixed upon her, she replied faintly, "Why, he looks quite . . . quite . . ."

"Exactly! He looks like the knavish renegade that he was. A regular thatch-gallows, I believe."

"Oh! How can you speak so of an ancestor who was very likely quite blameless?"

"Easily." Charles grinned. "It is no more than the truth, and why not? Not all of those fellows who came over with the Conqueror could have been Norman nobles. In fact, I believe Sir Charles received his baronetcy for his part in subduing the natives. And as you may have surmised, his reprehensible ways were passed on to some of his descendants. One of them even managed to lose the title. So you see, I come by my own less than admirable traits quite naturally."

Elizabeth blushed. "You are not so bad as that. You are not a . . ."

"A thatch-gallows?" He laughed. "Then your opinion of me is not so low, after all. I begin to have hope."

She glanced at him askance, but he merely took her arm, saying, "Shall we move on?"

As they made their way down the line of portraits, Elizabeth lost all sense of time, and it was not long before she knew that Charles was hoaxing her. He told such outrageous tales about every one of them that she began, laughingly, attempting to guess what crime he would attribute to each of his progenitors. She was so diverted, and it was so like past times with him, that it was not until they had almost reached the last of the line that she recalled Aunt Emily.

With a sudden rush of remorse, she cried, "Oh! What am I about? The doctor must long since have gone, and I must return to Aunt Emily."

Charles frowned, but did not attempt to dissuade her and politely escorted her to her aunt's bedchamber.

Elizabeth was amazed to discover the doctor still there, alone with his patient, for it had been well over an hour since he had come. Upon her entrance, however, the physician immediately took his leave, and Elizabeth, fearing that his lengthy stay meant that Aunt Emily's condition had worsened, followed him from the room.

But when she questioned him, the doctor replied soothingly, "No, no! As I told you, there is no cause for worry so long as she is not permitted to become overly distressed over anything."

After assuring him once more that she would not permit such an event, Elizabeth returned to her aunt's bedside to spend the remainder of the morning with her.

She had been sitting for nearly an hour, watching her aunt sleep and attempting, rather unsuccessfully, to divert her thoughts from Charles, when Aunt Emily's eyes fluttered open.

"You are here, my love?" she breathed. "So good of you. But you must not waste all your time in trying to amaze a sick old lady."

"Do not be absurd, Aunt Emily. You are nowhere near to being an old lady. And where else should I prefer to be, if not with you?"

"I had hoped..."

"Yes, well!" Elizabeth rushed into the breach. "How are you feeling, dearest?"

"Much better, my love. I am so sorry to have frightened you so."

"Nonsense! Only tell me what I can do to hasten your recovery."

Aunt Emily clutched her niece's hand. "Oh, Elizabeth, do you mean it? For there is something you can do which will make all the difference!"

With a feeling of dismay, but hoping that her suspicion was wrong, Elizabeth said, "Of course I mean it, Aunt Emily. I would do anything to help you. What is it you wish? Something special to tempt your appetite? Should you like me to read to you? What can I do to make you more comfortable?"

"Oh, my dear, if you truly wish to make me the happiest of creatures and quickly recovered, you will marry Charles!"

The colour drained from Elizabeth's face, and she could think of nothing to say for a moment, but then, cognizant of her aunt's delicate condition, and not wishing to worsen that condition, she said gently, "Aunt Emily, I promise you that I would do so if it were possible, but, indeed, it is not. You must know that it is not. Charles—"

She stopped speaking abruptly as Aunt Emily released her hand and raised her own to clutch at her chest, gasping for breath.

Elizabeth leapt from her chair and, leaning over her aunt, cried, "Oh, Aunt Emily! I will do anything! I will marry Charles! Only please, please do not die!"

Aunt Emily heaved a great sigh, and smiled radiantly at her niece. "There!" she exclaimed. "The pain is leaving me now."

Elizabeth sagged with relief and dropped back into her chair as the door burst open and Lady Langley rushed in, demanding, "What has happened? I thought I heard Elizabeth cry out!"

"Oh, Margaret—" Aunt Emily beamed "—I have the most wonderful news! Elizabeth has agreed to marry Charles!"

"Excellent! I shall inform him immediately," said her ladyship, turning to leave the room.

"No!" cried Elizabeth, reaching out as though to stop her.

"No?" asked Lady Langley, turning back again.

"No...that is, perhaps we should not be too precipitate. I mean..."

"Of course, my dear. I understand perfectly. You will wish to tell him yourself."

"Yes, I suppose so," agreed Elizabeth without conviction.

"You may find him in the library, my dear, and I shall remain here with Emily while you are gone, so you may take all the time you like."

"Oh, but there is no hurry!"

"Elizabeth?" came Aunt Emily's voice weakly. "You do not plan to change your mind again?"

"No, of course not, dearest," she answered, and seeing the distressed look on her aunt's face, she submitted to her fate and added, "Very well. I shall go and tell him now."

But how on earth was she going to do it? Elizabeth asked herself as she made her way slowly to the library. How humiliating to be obliged to beg Charles to marry her! For all her agonizing, however, by the time she reached her destination, she still had no clear notion of what to say to him.

As she entered the room, Charles took one look at her troubled countenance and came to her, taking her hands in his. "What is it?" he asked with concern. "It cannot be your aunt!"

"No... Well, yes, in a way it *is* Aunt Emily."

He looked annoyed. "What has she done now?"

"Charles!" Elizabeth exclaimed, shocked at his show of insensibility.

"No, no!" he declared, attempting to look contrite. "I meant to ask, what has happened to her?"

"Well, fortunately nothing irreparable. However, I fear that I caused her to become agitated and she very nearly had a set-back. You know that the doctor warned me of it."

"Yes, but she is better now?"

"Yes," Elizabeth said hesitantly.

"Then why are you still looking so harrowed?" he demanded.

Realizing suddenly that Charles had been holding her hands for the past several moments, Elizabeth tried to free them, but he only held them more tightly, and blushing, she lowered her eyes. "Well, you see, I only averted a more serious outcome by... by promising something to her."

"And?"

"Oh, dear. This is so difficult!"

He was silent for a moment, then asked, "Am I correct in assuming that this promise of yours involves me in some way?"

Her eyes flashed to his. "Oh, Charles, I tried to tell her that it was impossible, and I know how you will dislike it, but, truly, I could not deny her when she very nearly went into another dreadful spasm, and . . . and . . ."

His lips twitched almost imperceptibly as he said, "Come now, can you not tell me what this promise of yours is?"

"Will you marry me, Charles?" she blurted out. His eyes seemed to blaze for just an instant with an odd light, but unable to decipher its meaning, she rushed on. "It need not be for very long. As soon as Aunt Emily is well, we can obtain an annulment."

He released her hands, crossed his arms over his chest and eyed her with what looked suspiciously like amusement. "An annulment? We shall see. I have not yet accepted your offer, but it seems to me that if I am to help you keep this promise, I should be allowed the privilege of making the decisions regarding this proposed marriage."

"Certainly, whatever you wish," agreed Elizabeth with no clear notion of what it was that he wished. "I know I've no right to ask such a favour of you, but I should be so grateful!"

"And you will not cry off this time?"

"Oh, no!" she assured him.

"Very well, then," he said, bowing and kissing her hand. "Miss Ashton, I am cognizant of the great honour you do me, and I accept your marriage proposal."

He seemed to be taking the whole matter in a very light vein, but before she could decide how to answer him, he was leading her to the door, where he said, "I suggest that you return to your aunt and give her the good news while I take care of some pressing business. I have a great deal to do in a very short time."

"Oh, but shouldn't we discuss . . ."

He placed a finger over her lips, shaking his head slightly. "You must not argue with your husband-to-be, my dear."

"Well, I am not at all certain that I care for this tyrannical attitude of yours," she told him, frowning.

"Nevertheless, you will bear with it until after our marriage takes place. At that time, I give you permission to rip up at me all you wish."

And with that he gave her a small push in the direction of the stairs, but when she looked back at him, he was already striding out of the house.

In complete bewilderment, she climbed the stairs, but she had scarcely reached the top when Melanie met her, saying that Aunt Emily wished to be read to, and so Elizabeth returned to the library to select an appropriate book. When she finally entered her aunt's chamber once more, it was to find another surprise in store for her. The drapes had been drawn open, and in the light flooding through the windows, Aunt Emily sat propped up in bed. She looked the picture of health, her natural colour wholly restored.

"Aunt Emily!" Elizabeth exclaimed. "I can hardly credit how well you look!"

"Oh, yes, it is truly amazing how very well I feel, and it is all owing to you, my love. But I see you have brought a book with you. I shall just rest here while you read to me."

As Lady Langley excused herself, Elizabeth sat and proceeded to read to her aunt, and continued until a lunch tray was sent up for both of them. But afterwards, when the tray had been removed, she suggested that her aunt might like to sleep for a time. Aunt Emily denied this.

"Oh, no, my dear, for I am not at all tired!" she declared.

Looking at her aunt, whose colour seemed unnaturally heightened and whose eyes appeared unusually bright, Elizabeth said, "But, Aunt Emily, I do not wish you to become overly excited, and this is the longest you have remained awake since your illness began."

"Perhaps I should become sleepy if you were to read to me some more."

Hoping that it would indeed be so, Elizabeth reluctantly reached for the book, but before she could pick it up, the door opened, and Charles was there, ushering Lady Langley, Melanie, the doctor and a tall, thin stranger into the room.

"Charles!" Elizabeth exclaimed, not much caring at that moment whether she seemed rude. "I cannot think so much company is good for Aunt Emily just yet!"

"Oh, I rather think it will be the best curative in the world for her," he answered and, gesturing toward the tall, thin gentleman, he said, "I do not believe you have met the Reverend Mr. Simpson, my love. He is here to perform our wedding ceremony."

CHAPTER NINETEEN

ELIZABETH LOOKED at the beaming faces surrounding her with shock and consternation, as well as a feeling of being trapped, and lastly, staring at Charles, she said in a shaking voice, "Oh, no! We cannot! It is too soon!"

The smile faded from the lanky clergyman's rather unremarkable countenance and changed with ludicrous swiftness to disapproval laced with uncertainty and confusion. Turning to Charles he said, a trifle censoriously, "Indeed, sir, you did not tell me that the bride was reluctant. I really must decline to perform the ceremony if such is the case."

"Nonsense!" declared Lady Langley. "She is nothing of the sort!"

Aunt Emily queried tremulously, "Elizabeth?"

The good doctor stepped to Aunt Emily's bedside, took her hand in his and murmured soothingly, while Melanie merely stood by, observing the proceedings with great interest.

Charles moved to Elizabeth's side and led her over to a window embrasure, away from the others. "But how is this?" he asked in a low voice, one expressive eyebrow cocked mockingly. "Are you crying off after promising that you would not?"

"Of course not!" she hissed. "But you did not warn me of your intentions. I had not expected it to be so soon. There has been no time to prepare."

"What is it you need to prepare? I have the special license; the vicar is present, as are our family members. What more is necessary?"

"How can you ask such a foolish question? You are deliberately misunderstanding me! I...you have only to look at me! My gown and...and my hair. Oh, how could you?"

Charles leaned back and scanned her coolly from head to toe, then murmured, "Are you fishing for compliments, sweetheart? There is not a damned thing wrong with your appearance and if you think to back down at this stage of the game—don't! No, don't poker up on me! I have no intention of allowing you to renege on your promise."

"You are arrogant and insufferable!"

"Admittedly! I shall also be your husband quite soon."

They had been speaking in near whispers, and now the vicar's voice could be clearly heard. "I fear this is most irregular! I really believe that I must decline to perform my office unless both participants are quite willing."

One quelling glance from Charles silenced his protestations, but then Aunt Emily quavered, "Elizabeth?"

"Well?" demanded Charles.

But it was hearing Aunt Emily's voice that decided Elizabeth that she must accept defeat as gracefully as possible. Whatever her own feelings, she could not endanger her aunt's health and quite possibly her life.

"Very well," she said in a nearly normal tone of voice.

Several sighs were heard round the room as Charles took Elizabeth's arm to lead her back to Aunt Emily's bedside, where the clergyman awaited them. Smiling pleasantly, Charles leaned to say into the ear of his betrothed, "Smile! Anyone would think you were being led to the gallows."

As they took their places with the vicar standing before them, holding the small book that he carried, open in his hands, Elizabeth was smiling, but it felt stiff and unnatural. In truth, she felt much more like weeping, and she glanced up quickly at Charles's profile, noting the rigid set of his jaw. She had not meant to anger him, but oh! why could he not understand?

This was all so very wrong! Oh, not the fact that they were being married in a sickroom, or that she was wearing one of her oldest and plainest day gowns, or that there were none of the usual trappings. None of those things were important. She would gladly have married Charles in a cow byre wearing nothing other than her nightshift if only it were something that he wanted as much as she.

Nor had she been attempting to go back on her word. It was simply...but she didn't know what it was. She supposed that she had hoped to have more time to prepare herself, both mentally and emotionally, for this unconventional marriage. They had not even discussed the particulars of it. She did not know what to expect of it or of him.

The sound of the clergyman's voice had formed a background to her unhappy thoughts, and fragments of the wedding rite began to come through to her consciousness. *Dearly beloved...gathered here... this man and this woman...holy matrimony.* But now he was saying, "Repeat after me..."

And Charles was gazing intently into her eyes. "I, Charles, take thee, Elizabeth..."

He no longer looked angry, but it was impossible for Elizabeth to read his true thoughts or feelings from his enigmatic expression. She felt as if she might drown in the deep blue of his eyes, might listen to the sound of his voice forever and never tire of it.

And now it was her turn. "I, Elizabeth, take thee, Charles..."

She spoke her vows clearly, her eyes never leaving his, and she meant every word of them from the depths of her heart and soul. Whatever the future held in store for them, whatever a few legal papers might say, she would always consider herself married to Charles, joined to him for all time, until death parted them, and she hoped even beyond that.

And now Charles was claiming his bridal kiss; it was scarcely more than a soft touching of lips, lasting no more than a moment, and suddenly they were surrounded, with everyone laughing and offering congratulations. A glass of champagne was pressed into Elizabeth's hand.

In a daze, she looked down at the ring Charles had so recently placed on her finger. *With this ring I thee wed.* The words echoed through her mind. She was married to Charles, the love of her life, the keeper of her heart, though he might never know it. But for how long?

In an effort to shake off her sentimental mood, Elizabeth swallowed the entire contents of the glass of bubbling liquid she had been holding, and found it instantly refilled. Lady Langley was kissing her on both cheeks, exclaiming, "My dear, I cannot tell you how very pleased I am to call you sister!"

Good God! This did make them sisters. How very odd to think of Lady Langley in that light.

"Rather daunting, is it not?" came Charles's voice in her ear, and she glanced up swiftly to see the old teasing gleam in his eyes.

"You have been reading my mind," she replied with a laugh.

"Would that I could," he murmured.

But Melanie was beside Elizabeth, demanding her attention, embracing her and exclaiming, "Oh, this is famous! Now you shall be able to help launch me in the spring."

"Yes," agreed Elizabeth, smiling though a bitter-sweet pain stabbed at her heart. Would she be with Charles in the spring?

Her eyes were drawn to Charles where he stood talking quietly to the vicar, and she drank in his tall, lean form, his tight-fitting breeches and shining boots setting off long, muscular, but shapely legs; his coat moulded to broad shoulders that needed no padding; his handsome, aristocratic face that had become so very dear to her. Though his head was turned partially away from her, she could easily envisage those wonderfully deep blue eyes as they had gazed into hers during the ceremony, or crinkled with laughter as she had so often seen them. *My husband,* she thought with awe. This handsomely elegant man was her husband!

As though sensing her gaze upon him, Charles turned his head and smiled at her, but she averted her eyes quickly, turning back to Melanie. Good God! What was the matter with her? This marriage was merely one of convenience, and she had been in danger of forgetting that important fact.

"My dear niece," came Charles's lazy drawl from directly behind Elizabeth, startling her with its nearness, "you must pardon me for interrupting, but I'm sure you will not wish to deny me the pleasure of my lovely bride's company for a few minutes."

As he spoke, he moved to Elizabeth's side and placed his arm casually about her waist, ignoring her self-conscious attempt to step away, and pulling her closer.

"Oh, Uncle Charles," giggled Melanie, "as if you need ask."

He bowed formally to his niece and, shifting his hand to the small of Elizabeth's back, guided her to the window embrasure once more. There he braced one arm against the wall and, leaning towards her intimately, said, "And now, my love, we are well and truly tied."

Elizabeth blinked and swallowed nervously before reminding him, "But only until it is possible to obtain an annulment, when Aunt Emily is again well."

His eyes roamed over her face and he smiled slightly, but she was completely thrown off balance when he asked, as if she hadn't spoken, "Where would you like to go for our wedding trip?"

"Wedding trip?" she almost squeaked, unable to believe she had heard him correctly.

"Certainly!" He grinned. "It is the customary thing. I believe its purpose is to ensure that the new bride and groom may come to know each other more...ah, better...away from the distractions of everyday life."

"I know that!" she said indignantly. "But..."

"I should like to take you to a wonderful little chateau I know of in France, but since the little monster over there is not likely to allow it, have you another preference?"

She looked at him uncertainly. "Oh, but a wedding trip is not necessary in our case. Ours is not, after all, a true marriage."

The amusement in his eyes deepened. "No?" he asked softly. "'In the eyes of God and man...not to be put asunder.' I'd call that very real indeed."

At a loss for words and unwilling to permit herself to hope, she looked thankfully towards Aunt Emily, who was calling, "My dear child, come and let me wish you happy, for I am quite sure you have made me the very happiest of creatures!"

Charles frowned, but stepped aside, and Elizabeth moved obligingly to the bedside, where she leaned down to accept Aunt Emily's kiss.

Smiling fondly, she scanned her aunt's face, worried that so much excitement might have taxed her strength, but Aunt Emily glowed. Scarcely heeding her aunt's stream of disconnected exclamations, she reached out absently to touch a small patch of white near the hairline on her aunt's temple, then looked down at her finger where some of the stuff had come off on it. Her frown of puzzlement grew as she rubbed her thumb and finger together, not comprehending, for a moment, what it was. Then it gradually dawned upon her, and with it, the truth. It was face paint! Her eyes lifted to her aunt's in disbelief.

Aunt Emily had fallen silent and was watching her niece apprehensively.

As if sensing some dramatic change in the atmosphere of the room, all its occupants turned their faces towards the bed, then registered varying degrees of astonishment, consternation and chagrin as Elizabeth cried out in ringing tones, "You have tricked me again!"

CHAPTER TWENTY

EVERYONE SEEMED frozen into place for several interminable seconds, like a tableau, and the silence was a palpable thing until the vicar's voice acted as a catalyst.

"Oh, dear! Oh, dear!" he fretted. "I feared as much. This is not what I can like! This is most unusual!"

Released from their wary immobility, everyone began to move and speak at once, but it was Charles's voice that Elizabeth heard.

"Elizabeth!" he said authoritatively, moving towards her.

Elizabeth threw him one accusatory glance, lifted her skirts and ran from the room before he could reach her, not stopping until she had gained the sanctuary of her own chamber, where she slammed the door shut and turned the key in the lock.

Ignoring the pounding on the door and Charles's insistent demands that he be admitted, she began to pace, her arms folded tightly across her stomach as though she were cold. But in truth, she was not cold. She was consumed by all the resentments of the past week, which now rose up to take strong possession of her. She fed her sense of outrage by recalling his abominable treatment of her, the insults he had subjected her to, and this final deception the last straw.

But she could not ignore the sudden loud thud that followed an ominous silence. She whirled about as the door crashed open, and Charles strode into the room. He did not stop until he was so close he was almost touching her, looming over her, and before she could prevent herself, she took a hasty step back.

"Do not attempt to lock me out of your room again!" he commanded.

Her chin rose stubbornly. "Get out of my chamber!"

"I will not! I am your husband!"

"By trickery."

"By whatever means, I am still your husband!" His expression suddenly softened and he said, "Damn it, Elizabeth, let me explain!"

"The way you allowed me to explain at the inn?" she asked scathingly. "I believe you made it perfectly clear at that time what you thought of me. 'Another man's leavings' was it not? Only I was *your* leavings, blast you!"

His face flushed slightly but at a slight sound from the hallway, he said in a low, urgent voice, "We cannot talk here. Get your bonnet and pelisse. We are leaving."

She glared at him. "Have you lost all your senses? I am not going anywhere with you!"

"You are!" he declared with certainty, and grabbing her arm, he stalked over to the wardrobe, dragging her with him.

Throwing the doors wide, one hand still clamped on her arm, he located the garment he sought and began jamming her into it as though she were a recalcitrant child.

"Will you stop this?" she hissed.

He paid her no mind, but snatched a bonnet from the shelf, placed it firmly upon her head and began tying it under her chin.

"Hold still!" he warned when she tried to move away, and such was the tone of his voice that she obeyed him, though her eyes shot daggers at him.

Very well, she thought, she would go with him, but only so that they could have this out in private, and then she would demand that he bring her back and they could put an end to this sham marriage.

But her dignity was sorely threatened by having very nearly to run in order to keep up with his long strides as he pulled her along the hallway, past Aunt Emily's open doorway, where several shocked faces stared out at them, down the stairs and across the entry hall where an impassive butler held the door wide for them and out to a waiting carriage.

Fairly tossing her into it, Charles gave an order to the driver, then climbed in after her, and the coach lurched forward.

Elizabeth pushed back into her corner of the seat to be as far from him as possible, but he only moved closer. She glared at him mutinously, as she said coldly, "I want an annulment."

"And if I were to agree to that request, what would you do?"

"I would return to my former, uncomplicated life with Aunt Emily, of course." Her quiet, placid, boring life, her mind said traitorously.

Charles was shaking his head slowly, his eyes crinkling with amusement. "I think not, sweetheart. I believe Miss Godwin will soon be accepting an offer from the good Doctor Smithfield."

"Charles!" gasped Elizabeth, surprised into forgetting her sense of being ill-used. "Aunt Emily and Doctor Smithfield? No wonder he has been underfoot so often. Do you really think they will make a match of it?"

"Certainly! He is almost as besotted as I."

Her eyes had begun to sparkle with laughter, but now she recollected her reasons for being here, and she schooled her expression accordingly.

"You need not lie to me. I know very well why you married me," she told him.

"And why is that?"

"In order to satisfy your sense of honour because you had . . . had so thoroughly compromised me."

"If you honestly believe that, my girl, then you are not as perceptive as I had thought." Charles was turned partially towards her, with one arm along the back of the seat, and he lifted his other hand to brush a wayward curl from her temple. "Why do you suppose I went to such trouble to marry you when I had already explained that your reputation is intact and a marriage between us not necessary?"

"I don't know," she answered sulkily, then continued accusingly, "You insulted me unforgivably at the inn."

He sighed. "I know, my love. And I am most damnably sorry. Do you think you could find it in your heart to forgive me if I tell you that I was half out of my mind with jealousy?"

"You were?" she asked wonderingly.

"I was," he assured her, untying her bonnet, removing it and setting it aside.

"But if you lo— If you cared for me, why did you give up so easily the other day in the summer house? Why were you willing to let me go without an argument?"

"Because I thought it was what you wished," he told her, his hand playing idly with a curl lying on her nape.

"Oh." She shivered slightly. "Then what made you change your mind?"

"Actually, Margaret did," he answered, raising his other hand to trail his forefinger along the curve of her cheek. "She pointed out that I would be the world's worst fool if I did not fight to keep you."

"She did?" Elizabeth asked distractedly.

"Mmm," he murmured, his finger moving to trace her jawline. "She did."

"Oh!" Elizabeth gasped, her wits almost addled as his finger brushed along the outline of her lips with a butterfly touch.

"Elizabeth," he whispered into her ear, "I love you to the point of distraction."

"Oh, Charles," she murmured with a sigh, melting into his welcoming arms, her cheek resting against the comforting strength of his chest, "I love you, too—*beyond* distraction."

He chuckled. "I was rather hoping you did, my sweet."

After a moment, she raised her face to gaze into his eyes, a worried frown on her brow. She sighed despairingly. "Oh, Charles, it will not do. I shall make you a perfectly wretched wife."

"You must allow me to be the judge of that, my love."

"No, it is true! Please don't interrupt me. You see, I am aware that you are something of a rake, and . . . and I know that it is common practice for husbands to keep mistresses." Her eyes lowered to his cravat.

"I also know that a wife is supposed to pretend ignorance of such things. But I very much fear that I could not. If I should hear of one of your chères amies, or—" she had suddenly remembered Lady Sabina "—or, even worse, if I should meet your current mistress in some drawing room, I am afraid that I should cause the most dreadful scene. I am quite certain that I could never be a complacent wife."

"Well, I suppose that is something that I shall simply have to put up with, since I do not intend to be a complacent husband."

She glanced quickly up at him and then back at his cravat. "But it is not the same thing. No one thinks ill of a jealous husband. But a jealous wife... Oh, you would soon learn to hate me!"

"Hush!" he said, crooking his finger under her chin and lifting it so that she was once more looking into his eyes. "I could never hate you, and the question will not arise. You see before you a completely reformed rake. What need would I have of chères amies, or mistresses, when I shall have you? You see, I have never forgotten a certain magical summer night at Langley, or the innocent girl who came to me then. Do you know how often I have dreamed of her?"

She shook her head, blushing becomingly, but did not look away. Her eyes searched his deeply, then seemingly satisfied with what she saw there, she smiled mischievously. "And you will not mind having such a thoroughly compromised bride?"

He shook his head slowly. "I wouldn't have any other. Will you mind having such a thoroughly compromising husband?"

She shook her head slowly, just before his lips descended to hers in a thoroughly wonderful kiss.

® HARLEQUIN *Temptation* ®

Lovers Apart

**FOUR
CONTROVERSIAL
STORIES!
FOUR
DYNAMITE
AUTHORS!**

Don't miss the last book in the LOVERS APART miniseries,
April's Temptation title #344, YOUR PLACE OR MINE by Vicki
Lewis Thompson.

If you missed January title #332, DIFFERENT WORLDS by Elaine K. Stirling, February title
#336, DÉTENTE by Emma Jane Spenser or March title #340, MAKING IT by Elise Title and
would like to order them, send your name, address and zip or postal code, along with a
check or money order for $2.75 for title #332 and title #336 and $2.95 for title #340, plus
75¢ postage and handling ($1.00 in Canada) for each book ordered, payable to Harlequin
Reader Service, to:

In the U.S.	In Canada
3010 Walden Ave.	P.O. Box 609
Box 1325	Fort Erie, Ontario
Buffalo, NY 14269-1325	L2A 5X3

Please specify book title(s) with your order.
Canadian residents add applicable federal and provincial taxes.   LAP-4R

HARLEQUIN
Romance®

This May, travel to Egypt with Harlequin Romance's FIRST CLASS title #3126, A FIRST TIME FOR EVERYTHING by Jessica Steele.

A little excitement was what she wanted. So Josslyn's sudden assignment to Egypt came as a delightful surprise. Pity she couldn't say the same about her new boss.

Thane Addison was an overbearing, domineering slave driver. And yet sometimes Joss got a glimpse of an entirely different sort of personality beneath his arrogant exterior. It was enough that Joss knew despite having to work for this brute of a man, she wanted to stay.

Not that Thane seemed to care at all what his temporary secretary thought about him....

H A R L E Q U I N
American Romance®

THE ROMANCE THAT STARTED IT ALL!

For Diane Bauer and Nick Granatelli, the walk down the aisle was a rocky road....

Don't miss the romantic prequel to WITH THIS RING—

I THEE WED
BY ANNE McALLISTER
Harlequin American Romance #387

Let Anne McAllister take you to Cambridge, Massachusetts, to the night when an innocent blind date brought a reluctant Diane Bauer and Nick Granatelli together. For Diane, a smoldering attraction like theirs had only one fate, one future—marriage. The hard part, she learned, was convincing her intended....

Watch for Anne McAllister's I THEE WED, available *now* from Harlequin American Romance.

ITW